She hugged the afghan tighter. "It's just that every time you get close you . . . we . . ."

With a crooked grin on his face, he reached out and touched her cheek. "Yeah, I know. It's something, isn't it? The way you and I react to each other. Spectacular."

"It doesn't matter," she said quickly. "Now, why don't you call Maggie—"

"Why would I call one of your friends when you are completely filling up my mind? When you respond to my kisses with such fire . . ."

"I was just trying to help you out, do you a favor," she began, but he stopped her with a look, and pulled her close to him.

"Then do me a favor, Samantha." His voice was low and slightly rough. "Kiss me. *You* kiss *me*."

She remembered the way his lips felt on hers and the way she melted inside, and forgot everything but the touch and taste of his mouth. She couldn't deny it when the kiss was everything she wanted. *He* was everything she wanted. . . .

As he deepened the kiss, she threaded her fingers into his hair. "I like the way you kiss me," he said in a gruff mutter. "It's the same way I kiss you —like I can't get enough. . . ."

Loveswept ® 710

ONE ENCHANTED AUTUMN

FAYRENE PRESTON

BANTAM BOOKS
NEW YORK · TORONTO · LONDON · SYDNEY · AUCKLAND

ONE ENCHANTED AUTUMN

A Bantam Book / October 1994

If you would be interested in receiving protective vinyl covers for your Loveswept books,
please write to this address for information:

Loveswept
Bantam Books
P.O. Box 985
Hicksville, NY 11802

ISBN 0-553-44417-4

Published simultaneously in the United States and Canada

Bantam Books are published by Bantam Books, a division of Bantam Doubleday Dell
Publishing Group, Inc. Its trademark, consisting of the words "Bantam Books" and the
portrayal of a rooster, is Registered in U.S. Patent and Trademark Office and in other
countries. Marca Registrada. Bantam Books, 1540 Broadway, New York, New York
10036.

PRINTED IN THE UNITED STATES OF AMERICA

OPM   0 9 8 7 6 5 4 3 2 1

ONE

She came toward him out of the sun. He lifted his hand to shield his eyes from the bright light. The tactic worked. As she walked briskly along the sidewalk in front of the Dallas courthouse, she gradually came into focus.

The November day was crisp and cool with gold, brown, and russet leaves on the trees. Amazingly her hair was the color of the leaves, russet with streaks of gold. It was pulled back into a chic French twist, and she wore a smart suit the color of her hair and the leaves.

He waited until she was a few feet away. "Excuse me. Are you Samantha McMillan?"

She stopped and looked at him with composed, deliberate assessment. Her eyes, he saw, were brown with touches of gold. Like the leaves.

"Yes. May I help you?"

He held out his hand to her. "I'm Matthew Stone, Leona Paterson's nephew."

Recognition flickered in her eyes. She reached out and shook his hand. "May I help you?"

It was the second time she had asked the question. She was obviously accustomed to people coming to her with problems. Understandable, he supposed, since she was a divorce lawyer. However distasteful he thought her profession, he had been told she was very good at what she did.

"I'd like to talk to you about my aunt and this proposed upcoming marriage of hers."

Just for a moment humor flashed across her face. In the bright autumn sunlight her fair complexion showed golden undertones, a faint smattering of freckles, and no discernible flaws.

"*Proposed* marriage, Mr. Stone? The last I heard Leona's wedding was set for the weekend after next. I plan to go and I assume you do too."

He shifted, like a boxer trying to find the best stance with which to face his opponent. "No, I don't and that's what I'd like to talk to you about."

"About the fact that you're not going? Leona will be crushed if you don't."

She had a firm grasp on a brown leather

briefcase, and a slim russet leather purse hung from her shoulder. As she impatiently tapped the toe of one leather shoe against the leaf-strewn sidewalk, and glanced at the practical gold-and-leather watch on her wrist, she seemed to him as cool and sharp as the day.

"I have to be in court in twelve minutes. I'm sorry, but—"

"Then tell me when."

"When what?"

"When you'll have time to talk to me."

She shifted her briefcase from one hand to the other. She knew who Matthew Stone was, not only because she was friends with his aunt but because he was a celebrated and award-winning investigative reporter. Just last year he had broken one of the biggest stories of the year about Peter Norton, Jr., a leading citizen of Dallas, and the story had had a nationwide impact.

He might want to talk to her about a family wedding, but she had the dead-certain feeling he was seeing her through the eyes of an investigative reporter rather than considering her as a friend of the family. Too bad, she thought objectively. Those eyes were nice, deep blue with an unusual intensity that was positively arresting. He also had nice hair, brown gleaming with copper lights, and a high, intelligent forehead. If she had more time, she might be able to come up with the name of one of her friends who would enjoy meeting him, but as it was . . .

Her beeper went off. He automatically checked his.

"It's mine," she murmured, fishing it from her purse and glancing at the number. "I don't have any time, Mr. Stone, at least not soon, and quite frankly I don't see any point in discussing your aunt's wedding. It's got nothing to do with me or even for that matter you."

He took a step closer to her. No doubt, she thought, it was an intimidation tactic, unconscious or otherwise, but it didn't even occur to her to back away.

"That's where you're wrong. I'm Leona's only living relative, and you, Ms. McMillan, are the person who introduced my aunt to this gigolo who thinks he's going to marry her. I want to know your angle—what's in it for you?"

Her mouth tightened as she again glanced at her watch. "I'm due in court in eight and a half minutes, plus I have a call to return, but just for your own general information, Mr. Stone, you seem to have several of your facts wrong. However, I have no time, much less the inclination, to tell you which facts or give you any explanations. Have a very nice day."

He didn't try to stop her, but he did turn to watch as she raced up the courthouse steps.

The wind sent leaves tumbling after her, but it failed to coax even a hair loose from her ever-so-efficient French twist. Quite an interesting lady, he mused. Far more interesting than he had expected.

The russet-colored suit fit her with precision. The jacket nipped in at her narrow waist, and the slim skirt skimmed in a neat line down over the slight swell of her hips to just above her knees. The suit was entirely proper, too proper for his own personal tastes.

Still he would see her again, he thought, though not at the wedding. There would be no wedding.

He glanced at his own watch and grimaced. He was due across town in twenty minutes at an appointment of his own. He started off, but suddenly stopped and again looked up at the courthouse doors through which she had disappeared. Yes, he thought, he would definitely see her again.

Matthew Stone was waiting for her when Samantha arrived back at her office at five that afternoon. She wasn't entirely surprised to see him lounging in her reception room, reading a news magazine. *Determined* and *relentless* were just two of the words she had heard used to describe him. And she had to admit she was becoming more and more curious about why he had turned that laser intensity of his on her because of a simple wedding.

She closed the outer door of her office behind her and crossed to her secretary, a stylish forty-year-old with a sharp mind and even sharper wit. "Hi, Barbara. Anything going on?"

Barbara threw a meaningful glance at the waiting man. "Just the usual—mayhem, chaos, and the occasional plague of locusts." She indicated a thick folder of documents on the corner of her desk. "These are ready for your reading enjoyment and signature, and your messages are on your desk."

She scooped up the folder with her free hand. "Thanks. Anything else?"

"There is just one more thing." She indicated Matthew with a wave of a manicured hand. "Mr. Stone is here to see you. He says it's personal."

"Does he now?" She turned around and discovered the full brunt of his dark blue eyes focused on her. Nice eyes, she thought once again. Eyes that would rivet some and intimidate others. As for herself she was mildly interested in why he had decided that she was involved in whatever was bothering him. "How long have you been here?"

"Not long. I figured late afternoon might be the best time of the day to catch you, unless of course you have a dinner meeting this evening. Or a date."

The man was beginning to amuse her. He reminded her of a patient bulldog, albeit an attractive bulldog. A quick mind scan of her friends lacking mates produced no one who needed someone with the qualities of a patient bulldog. Pity. After all, he was single, gainfully employed, and heterosexual, three sterling attributes his aunt had mentioned to her more than once. *Sterling*, Leona had emphasized.

He had drawbacks of course. She was sure she hadn't yet discovered all of them, but a few she'd already experienced firsthand. For instance she didn't particularly care for his in-your-face, abrasive manner. Still she hated to let such potentially good mate material go to waste without trying to match him up with at least one of her friends.

"Do I have a dinner meeting, Barbara?"

"Uh . . ." Barbara made a dutiful show of checking the appointment calendar. "Not unless you've made an appointment I don't know about."

"I can't remember." She knew her schedule down to the last five-minute increment, and so did Barbara. "I'll have to think about it. In the meantime"—she looked at Matthew—"perhaps I can spare a few minutes. Come in." She waved him into her office, then paused at the door and looked back at her secretary. "Have a great weekend."

"You don't need me to stay?" Barbara asked, her voice filled with hopefulness.

Samantha grinned. "No. I'll see you Monday."

Her office didn't surprise Matthew. It was as coolly efficient and crisply elegant as she was. The office took up a corner on the fortieth floor of a glass-and-steel high-rise that overlooked downtown Dallas, and it was furnished in polished mahogany, glistening crystal, and burgundy leather.

He chose one of the wing-backed leather chairs in front of the desk and sat down. "The divorce business obviously pays very well," he said, his tone deliberately confrontational.

Settled behind her desk, she began to sort through her messages, the slight arch of a brow her only reaction. "Are you interested in changing professions? If so, you might want to check with Barbara. I frequently give career talks at the neighborhood elementary schools. Maybe you could drop by and catch one of them."

"Thank you, Ms. McMillan, but being a divorce lawyer scores very low on my scale of career choices."

"Really?" Her tone was one of polite interest. "Even lower than snooping into other people's lives and systematically tearing them apart?"

"I only destroy people who deserve it. Can you say the same?"

She paused in her methodical reading and categorizing of the notes and glanced over at him. "By the time the majority of my clients come to me, their marriages are already shattered and they are ready to begin rebuilding their lives. In addition—"

"Oh, in addition? There's *more*?"

"In addition I don't make the call of who does or doesn't deserve to be destroyed. You, on the other hand, are obviously into God-like decisions."

"You flatter me, Ms. McMillan."

"Not at all, Mr. Stone. Not at all. Now, exactly what can I do for you this afternoon?"

"There's that question again."

"What question?" She made a note to herself on one of the messages, then pushed aside the small stacks she had made and drew the folder to her.

"You keep asking what you can do for me."

"That must be because I don't understand why you want to talk to me."

Beneath the desk she eased off her shoes and wiggled her tired feet. On top of the desk she reached for a gold ballpoint and began scanning the documents and letters one by one, then quickly signing them.

He spread out his hands. "I don't know how I can make myself any clearer."

"Why don't you give it a shot," she suggested sweetly, too sweetly.

He sent her a hard look, which, he noticed, was completely lost on her because she was once again bent over her work, her movements precise and efficient. If he undressed her, would he find equally precise and efficient angles, or would he find soft, womanly curves? It was an interesting question. Tantalizing, really.

Hours after he had first met her, her hair remained perfect in its French twist. Even inside under unnatural light its color reminded him of autumn leaves. He wondered what it would remind him of if he were to see her in winter. Or in spring.

"Ms. McMillan—"

She flinched; her head jerked up. She had been all too aware of his scrutiny of her. His gaze had felt as if it had slid past her skin, invaded her flesh, and gone straight to her bone. "Look, I don't know about you, but it's at the end of a long day that's at the end of a long week, and I'm getting tired of this 'Ms. McMillan, Mr. Stone' stuff. Call me Samantha. Your aunt does."

"I know she does."

Something in the utter softness of his voice made her lay down her pen and reach for the bottle of aspirin she kept in her top drawer. No, she immediately corrected herself, tossing the aspirin back and chasing it with a glass of water, it couldn't have been his voice. It had simply been a hell of a week.

"In fact," he continued, "since the two of you met at a charity affair just a few months ago, you've grown very close to her. I find that unusual."

"And I find your reaction unusual." She replaced the aspirin bottle in the drawer, folded her hands atop the gleaming mahogany desk, and waited. For the aspirin to take effect. And for his next volley. The volley came first.

He smiled.

She recognized a disarming tactic when she saw one, and in this case, she acknowledged, it was a powerful tactic. His smile was warm, sympathetic, and sensual. . . .

"How's your headache?" he asked, his voice low and amazingly soothing.

Only minutes before, she had viewed him as abrasive. Now he was smooth as cream. "I don't have one."

"Then why the aspirin?"

"Because I don't want a headache."

"How extremely efficient of you to stop a headache before you get one."

She glanced at her watch. "Please cut to

the chase and simply come right out and tell me what it is you want to know."

"Samantha . . ."

He paused for a moment as if he were savoring the sound of her name. Another tactic, she was sure, intended to unnerve. She regarded him impatiently.

"Samantha, I'm very concerned about my aunt."

"Why? She's extremely happy. She and Alfred are very much in love."

He still smiled, but his blue eyes narrowed slowly, and he gazed at her with the same intensity a cobra might view an opponent right before it strikes. "From what I've gathered from my aunt, you introduced her to this Alfred Trevarthen, who is supposedly a friend of yours."

"Not supposedly—he *is* a friend of mine." She again glanced at her watch. "Is this going to take much longer?"

"Why? Have you remembered a dinner date?"

"Yes, I have and I can't miss it." It was with her mom and her mom's second husband, David.

"It's an important date, then?"

"I wouldn't have made the date in the first place if it wasn't. My time is very important to me—time, I might add, which you are currently wasting."

"Perhaps if I offered to pay you for your time . . . Is that what Trevarthen did? Pay you to hook him up with my aunt?"

She stiffened. "I don't charge my friends, and Alfred is my friend. As for you, Mr. Stone, you couldn't afford me."

"Try me."

"Sorry, I pick and choose both my friends and my clients. You're neither. Are we nearly through?"

He didn't move, but his posture seemed to change. The cobra was gone, and in its place a tiger lazed contentedly in the noonday sun. It was as if he had just consumed a large meal and now had all the time in the world to digest it. The meal hadn't been her, she was sure. She would definitely notice if he took so much as a small bite out of her, and he hadn't. What he *had* done in the space of a very short time was remind her of three different animals. She'd been right the first two times, and she didn't expect to be proven wrong about the third.

He crossed his legs and gazed thoughtfully down at his joined hands. "I'll try not to take up too much more of your valuable time. I'd just like to understand why a woman of your age—by the way, may I ask how old you are?"

"No, you may not."

He shrugged and stroked a hand down the side of his jaw. "Okay, no problem. I'll guess thirty-two. Maybe even thirty-four. No, wait—"

"Thirty," she said in a biting tone.

His smile widened. "Thank you. Thirty. Then why would a young woman such as yourself want to spend time befriending a woman who's so much older?"

"What's age got to do with it?" she asked, genuinely puzzled. "Your aunt's an extremely nice lady and very easy to like. Don't you like her?"

"I *love* her. She was like a second mother to me when my own died. That's why I'm trying to figure this whole thing out and why I'm also trying to understand why you, an obviously busy career woman, would want to go to the time and effort to fix my aunt up with a stranger?"

"He isn't a stranger to me, and now he isn't a stranger to Leona. He seems to be a stranger only to you."

His expression was pleasant and his voice remained soft. "Alfred Trevarthen *is* a stranger to me, but my aunt isn't. She's sixty-six years old, Samantha, and she's worked hard all her life to earn the financial security she currently enjoys. I'm not going to sit idly by and watch that jeopardized."

He was now handling her with kid gloves, but strangely enough for the first time she noticed his confidence and masculinity. It had always been there of course, but she supposed she had been focusing on other things, such as his eyes and what he wanted from her. Maybe she did have a friend she could match him up with after all. She'd have to give the matter some more thought. Perhaps Maria Keaton . . .

"I'm sorry, but if there's a point here, I'm afraid I'm missing it."

He smiled again. "Ah, come on, Samantha. Don't disappoint me now. You're getting it just fine."

Beneath the desk she slid on her shoes, crossed her legs, then settled back in her chair. "You know, Matthew, you're really very good. Honestly. I'm sure if I think about it long enough, I'll feel privileged that you thought me important enough to make me the focus of all that charm, intensity, and intellect of yours. But the problem, you see, is that it's all going to waste. You should save it for some other hapless person whose life you deem needs exposing."

His brows shot up. "Hapless person? Where did that attitude come from? Have I done an investigative piece on one of your friends? Norton perhaps?"

"No. Actually I have no quarrel with the work you did on him. He had a lot of power, and it would have been a disaster if he'd gotten more. Mainly I was speaking in general."

"I don't suppose there was a compliment in there somewhere?"

"You don't strike me as a man who needs compliments."

"And you, Samantha, don't strike me as a woman who does things without a motive. So let's get back to my original question: Why did you fix my aunt up with this man I've never heard of? What's in it for you?"

For the first time she smiled at him, but it wasn't a true smile, and she was sure he knew it. "Nothing but the simple joy of seeing two people happy."

His own smile faded as he suspiciously eyed hers. "You're leading me in circles, and I don't like the feeling."

She shrugged. "If you're going to persist in asking these stupid questions, then I'd say you'd better get used to the feeling."

He exhaled a long breath. "Okay, Samantha, I'm going to give you the benefit of the doubt here—"

"*Sure* you are."

He ignored her comment. "Perhaps you don't know, but my aunt has a long history of bad relationships."

"I wouldn't exactly call four marriages in sixty-six years a long history."

"Of course you wouldn't. You're a divorce attorney."

"Her first two marriages weren't bad relationships. She was widowed both times."

"And both deaths left her devastated."

"And that's what you call a bad relationship?"

"The end result was the same—she was hurt. And the other two marriages ended in divorces that enabled each man to walk away with considerably fatter pockets than he had before. Besides the marriages there were a few other close calls that required my intervention. I don't want to see it happen again. I want to protect her."

She eyed him deliberately. He was wearing slacks made of heavy-duty khaki, a plaid shirt of blue, tan, and rust, a smoky blue knit tie knotted carelessly at his neck, and a fawn-colored corduroy jacket. The jacket had suede patches at the elbows. On some men the touch might seem pretentious, but on him it appeared perfectly natural because the patches were slightly worn as if he spent a lot of time with his elbows resting on a desk. On his feet were brown leather boots, well broken in. Masculine, she thought again. Some might say overpoweringly so. She didn't think he'd suit Maria Keaton after all.

"Tell me something, Matthew. By the way, may I call you Matthew?"

He nodded. "By all means. Anyone who

can lead me in circles should feel free to call me Matthew."

"No one is leading you in circles. You just keep making left turns, and *radical* left turns at that. So *stop* it and tell me why you would automatically jump to the conclusion that Alfred is a gold digger? You haven't even met him yet."

"I just told you. My aunt has a terrible track record with men. Her judgment hasn't always been what it should be. She's known Trevarthen only a little over a month, and she's told me, I might add, that the man is a part-time greeter at a discount department store."

"What's wrong with that? It's good, honest work."

"What's wrong with it is that Leona will be supporting him. And one other thing. I've made several attempts to meet this man, and each time he's given me an excuse as to why he couldn't come."

"Maybe his excuses were legitimate."

"And maybe they weren't."

She picked up her gold pen and impatiently tapped it on the desk. "So why aren't you investigating him?"

"I've been on a deadline and haven't had a lot of time, but when I've had a few minutes here and there, I have tried to check him out.

Unfortunately I haven't been able to find out anything, and now he's out of town."

"*What?* He had the nerve to leave town without asking your permission? And you haven't found any criminal record? What about parking tickets? Perhaps you haven't looked in the right places. If I were you, I'd keep looking. In fact spend all your time digging into Alfred's past. Dig so much that you forget to talk to Leona and see what it is that she really wants. And refuse to go to the wedding—that would be good too. You'd really be protecting her then, wouldn't you?" She couldn't remember any other man being able to wind her up so tightly.

His eyes turned to blue ice. "Think what you like about me, but I won't stop until I'm satisfied."

Tiring of the game they were playing, she tossed the pen down onto the desk. "And what exactly is it going to take to satisfy you, Matthew? Everything I've told you has been the truth, but, okay, I'll elaborate. You keep mentioning your aunt's judgement? A few mistakes in sixty-six years? We should all have such a good track record. And as for Alfred—who, by the way, is sixty-eight and not stupid either—I had known him for about a year when I met Leona a few months ago. I thought about it for a while and decided they would be a perfect match. I was right. I introduced them last month, and now they're going to get married in two weeks and live happily ever after. End of story. That's it. *Deal* with it, Matthew."

He stared at her, his features stone hard, his words even harder. "I don't think so. No, Samantha, I don't think so at all."

Silently uttering an oath, she glanced around her desk to see if there was something else she needed to do before she left. There were the messages. Two she would return from her mom's home. The others could wait until Monday.

"People lie to me all the time," he said. "Why should I believe you?"

She looked back at him and, without knowing why, decided to take one more shot at making him understand. "Because, Matthew, sometimes people *do* tell the truth, and you're too good a reporter not to know that. Your problem is you have a job that demands intense concentration and, I'm sure, keeps you on the run. And then one day out of the blue your aunt tells you she's marrying someone you don't know and that she was introduced to that person by another person you don't know. The timing seems awfully fast. You panic. Leona is your aunt. You love her. You want to protect her. You can't find Alfred because he's out of town and so you track me down, the person you see as culpable in this matter. So far that's all commendable. The problem is your vision is currently not extending beyond the end of your nose."

"Is that a fact?" His gruff tone was laced with sarcasm.

"Oh, *stuff* it!"

"Stuff it, counselor? Is that some sort of legal term?"

"In this case it's definitely an *appropriate* term. Look, I'm tired and I need to get out of here. So just listen. Take a deep breath, relax, go talk to your aunt—"

"I can't."

She blinked. "Why not?"

He focused on a small crystal pig that sat on the corner of her desk. It was the only touch of whimsy in an otherwise strictly businesslike atmosphere. He reached for it and absently examined it. "Because she's mad at me."

"Mad at you? Why?"

He sighed. "Because I told her I wasn't going to let her marry this Alfred guy." He stared at the pig and waited. When she didn't say anything, he lifted his head and looked across the expanse of mahogany at her.

She spread her hands out. "I'm speechless."

He returned the pig to the desk with an alarming thud and surged to his feet. "Good. Stay that way. It's a nice change."

She glanced at her pig to make sure it was still in one piece. "Where are you going?"

"I've got dinner plans too."

"Oh." She hadn't considered the possibility that he might be seeing someone. She had assumed since Leona hadn't mentioned anyone . . . She pushed to her feet, walked around to the front of her desk, and leaned back against it. "So what are you going to do about Leona and Alfred? If you made Leona mad, you must have said or done something colossally stupid."

"Thanks a lot."

She crossed her arms beneath her breasts. "That wasn't as big an insult as it sounds. It's just that I know Leona. She doesn't get mad easily."

"It *was* a big insult, but I probably deserve it. You're right about Leona. She's a sweetheart." Slipping his hands into the pockets of his slacks, he strolled over to one of the windows and gazed out at the now-dark sky. The skyscrapers of Dallas were lit up, and below him on the freeway cars streamed past in a blur of lights that resembled glittering ribbons strewn in different directions. Soon he'd be down there, part of one of the ribbons. He wished he hadn't agreed to the dinner meeting, but he hoped the information he would receive would be the final piece in an investigative puzzle he had been working on for weeks. Then he could turn his full attention to Joe Gates, a man who had recently contacted him and made several tantalizing statements. He was eager to meet with him. If he was lucky, Gates would be the beginning of a trail that would provide him with a lot of answers about one possibly crooked judge.

Samantha eyed the broad line of his shoulders with resignation. Was it her imagination, or did he seem as tired as she felt? "Are you free tomorrow night?"

He turned around. "For what?"

"For dinner at my house. I'll invite Leona and Alfred—he'll be back in town by then—and we'll get this matter straightened out once and for all."

His brows rose, causing his forehead to furrow. "Why would you do that?"

"You're right about Leona. She is a sweetheart. That's why I'm finding it hard to believe you really are her nephew, but that's beside the point. Even though you have *strongly* suggested that I'm probably getting some sort of kickback from introducing Alfred to Leona, and you've stopped just short of saying the word *collusion* and maybe even *procurement*, I'm still going to do this, for Leona's sake." She turned to her desk and scribbled her home address on the back of one of her business cards, then handed it to him. "Seven o'clock, Matthew. Be there. If you're not, it will be your loss."

"Oh, don't worry, Samantha. I'll be there."

TWO

It was raining when Matthew pulled up in front of Samantha's house the next evening at five minutes before seven.

He had expected her address to be a condominium in a high-rise much like her office, or perhaps one of the many new high-six-figure homes in and around Dallas. He expected it to be done in luxurious fabrics and cool colors, with huge windows providing spectacular views of the city, trendy art on the walls, and a catered meal served in an elegant dining room on fine china.

But he received a surprise. Her home was a relatively small, wooden, one-story house with an old-fashioned wraparound front porch furnished with white wicker that invited leisure and repose. Mums were planted in the flower beds, and pansies grew in the window boxes. An orange, gold, and russet wreath made up of leaves and ribbons adorned the front door.

He double-checked the address before he rang the bell, then waited impatiently. His dinner the night before had gone well. All the article needed now was a few finishing touches, and then he could turn his attention to Joe Gates. The story Gates had hinted at had all the makings of a blockbuster, and he could hardly wait to get started on it. But first he had to take care of this sixty-eight-year-old Romeo who had managed to attach himself to his aunt.

His adrenaline was pumping. He was looking forward to tonight. He already had Alfred Trevarthen's measure. The task that faced him in the next few hours was to get Leona to see the man as he saw him, an elderly guy tired of living off his Social Security and looking for a woman with a bank account big enough to ensure that his golden years would be truly golden. He didn't think it would be that hard to discredit the man.

The person he remained curious about was Samantha. Samantha with the cool, brisk demeanor and hair and eyes the color of autumn leaves. Samantha . . .

She opened the door, a welcoming smile on her face. "Good evening, Matthew. Please come in."

He blinked and looked again. And he saw an entirely different woman from the one he had met yesterday.

She stepped back, and keeping his gaze glued on her, he entered.

Everything about her had changed, softened. Her hair lay loose over her shoulders, the russet and gold strands brushed to a gleaming shine. She wore a ginger-colored chiffon dress that reached down to her ankles. A beige slip showed through the sheer material, the flowers in its pattern appearing as if through a mist.

She moved away from him, down the hall, and into another room, her feet in ballet slippers, the hem of her dress drifting out around her. He trailed after her, following the scent of spices, honey, and vanilla.

"Alfred and Leona called. They'll be a few minutes late. Would you like a glass of wine while we're waiting?"

He nodded. He couldn't take his eyes off her. She looked fragile and womanly, all soft curves and enchanting femininity.

She handed him a wineglass filled with a golden rose liquid. "It's strawberry wine. I made it myself. If you'll excuse me, I need to check on something in the kitchen. Just make yourself at home."

He sipped the wine. It tasted delicate and faintly sweet with a subtle hint of something

magical—just as Samantha appeared tonight.
He looked around the room and discovered
hardwood floors waxed to a rich gloss, a fire
that crackled warmly in a brick-and-stone fireplace, and furniture with plump cushions and
needlepoint pillows. Lace curtains hung at the
windows, and a hand-crocheted afghan lay
across a large, round ottoman. This couldn't
be the home of the woman he had met yesterday.

Taking the wine with him, he went into
the kitchen. She was stirring a big pot of
something that made his mouth water just
smelling it.

"Are you hungry?" She pointed to a tall
butcher-block table and a bowl of finely
chopped marinated vegetables surrounded by
wheat crackers. "Help yourself. The vegetables came from my garden."

He scooped up a portion and popped it in
his mouth. It was delicious.

"Pour yourself some more wine."

He did, then drank as he took in the
kitchen. Bundles of rosemary and mint hung
amid copper pots on a rack suspended from
the ceiling. A window box on the counter behind the sink held basil. By the stove a hook
held a fragrant, exuberant wreath of bay
leaves. Dangling from it by a dark green gros-
grain ribbon was a pair of small scissors.
Through the glass doors of her cupboards he

could see jars of canned pickles, squash, beets, and carrots. Here and there braids of onions, garlic, red chilis, and dried flowers trailed down the walls.

He sank onto a stool beside the table. Somewhere in the house Harry Connick, Jr., crooned. Outside, the rain fell, pattering against the roof and the windows. Inside, Samantha, so different from the brisk lawyer he had met yesterday, was quite simply overwhelming him.

"How do you like the wine?"

He hadn't spoken yet, he realized. Not a word. "It's very good. You said you made it?"

She smiled, a genuine smile. "Yes. It's a hobby of mine."

The effect of her smile on him was as head-spinning and befuddling as any wine he'd ever had. "I've never met anyone before who makes her own wine."

"It's not that unusual. Besides, it's not as if I've got a winery going here. But every year or so if the berries are very good, I'll make wine. And jam."

Wine and jam. She made her hobby sound so commonplace. "And you grow vegetables too?"

"Along with other things."

In an effort to regain his equilibrium he attempted to shift gears mentally. "Your garden must be one for the books. The plants are probably time efficient, with no weeds or slacking off allowed."

Her smile never faltered. "Is there any other kind of garden?"

"Not for you, I wouldn't think." She didn't react. Eyeing her with a frown, he sipped the wine. It was then that he noticed she wasn't wearing a watch. "What did you say before about my aunt?"

"Oh, they're running a little late. Since it's Saturday, Alfred worked a few more hours than he usually does. They should be here soon. Have some more of the vegetables."

He trowled a wheat cracker through the appetizing mixture. "Is this really your house?"

"What a funny question. Whose house do you think it is?"

"I don't know. Maybe your evil twin's?"

"Evil?" She glanced over her shoulder at him and barely prevented a start. His expression was slightly perturbed, but since she knew how he felt about Alfred, she wasn't surprised. What did surprise her was how natural he looked in her kitchen, as natural as the herbs and vegetables that she had grown, as natural as if somehow he, too, had been grown organically right where he sat. He didn't appear ill at ease with the surroundings, only puzzled about something as he drank her wine and ate her vegetables. He was clearly a man comfortable in his own skin. And he possessed a natural earthiness that amazingly matched the ambience of her kitchen. He was very attractive, she thought. "Evil?" she said again, fearful of losing track of the conversation.

"Well, maybe not evil, but certainly not your divorce-lawyer twin. You have to admit this house is about as different from your office as the ocean is from the desert. And that goes for you too. You're not the same person you were yesterday."

"Of course I am."

"No, Samantha, you're not."

She turned around so that she could see him better. "The only difference is that tonight I'm at home instead of at work."

"No, it's more than that. You're *completely* different."

Her brow knitted, and she wiped her hands on a dishtowel. "I don't know what to tell you except that this is the way I live when I'm not at work."

He wasn't satisfied. Yesterday he had seriously wondered whether he'd find sharp angles if he undressed her. Tonight he knew he'd find nothing but softness. And tonight he definitely wanted to undress her. In fact the thought was crowding everything else out of his mind.

She passed by him, and he caught a scent of cinnamon and vanilla mixed with other intriguing spices. And honey, definitely honey. Feeling slightly dizzy, he lifted the wineglass and drank. The wine, he realized, was more intoxicating than he had originally thought. Like her. Who was Samantha McMillan? The question fascinated him.

His job was to ferret out inconsistencies, and Samantha was one huge inconsistency. She bothered him even though he knew he shouldn't let her. She wasn't a news story, and after tonight he wouldn't even be seeing her again. But, dammit, she intrigued him.

Back at the oven she bent and took out two perfectly browned loaves of homemade bread. "So tell me, Matthew, are you currently seeing anyone, seriously or otherwise?"

He paused in the act of pouring himself another glass of wine. "Excuse me?"

She placed the loaves of bread into baskets and covered them with dark-red-and-cream-colored gingham cloth. "I asked if you were involved with anyone?"

"Why? Are you propositioning me?"

"Hardly. I have several friends who might be right to introduce you to, that's all."

"Why would you want to do that?" he asked blankly.

She shrugged. "It's a hobby of mine."

He didn't know whether it was the wine's effect on him or the way she was phrasing her

sentences, but he was having trouble under-
standing her. "What is?"

"Matchmaking."

"You're kidding."

"Not at all. I'm very good at it. Most of
my matches end in marriages."

Another inconsistency. "But you make a
living from *dissolving* marriages."

"Only those that can't be repaired."

He stared at her. "You're really serious,
aren't you?"

"Absolutely."

"And that's why you introduced my aunt
to this Alfred character? Because you believe
you're good at *matchmaking*?" He sat his
wineglass down and pushed it away from him.
He'd obviously had too much.

"They're going to be very happy together.
I'm rarely wrong, which is why I think I could
find you someone. I know a really lovely person you might have a lot in common with.
She's a free-lance writer. Mainly she does
product brochures and publicity releases, but
she's also published several short stories." She
gnawed on her bottom lip and contemplated
his expression, which suggested he thought
horns had suddenly grown from her head.
"Well, okay, so that's not exactly the type of
writing you do, but it is still writing, right?
Oh, and she loves romantic movies. Do you?"

"Only if it involves car chases, car crashes, and cars exploding."

"Action-suspense, huh?" She shrugged. "Martha probably wouldn't have been right for you anyway. Let me see . . . oh, I know, Freda Jackson—she's an accountant. Very successful too. She has her own business. She might enjoy counting demolished cars. And she loves horses."

"I'm allergic to them."

"Oh, well, she probably wouldn't have been right for you either. Do you like any kind of sport? I know someone who—"

"I'm *not* interested."

"Oh, come on, Matthew. There's not a person alive who wouldn't want to be matched up with exactly the right person for them."

"What about you?"

"Me?"

He nodded, feeling infinitely more comfortable asking the questions rather than answering them. "Have you found the right person for you?"

"I'm not the topic of conversation here."

"As a matter of fact you are. I just made you the topic by asking if you'd found the right person. And I think it's a reasonable question, too, since you were trying to convince me of your matchmaking abilities."

"Look, you can believe me or not. It

doesn't matter. I was only trying to help you out a little."

For a moment he thought he caught the impatient tone of the lawyer he had met yesterday, but then he realized she was reacting far too casually. If it were yesterday and they were in her office, she would have been tapping her pen or drumming her fingers. But tonight in her home she merely shrugged.

And he didn't like her treating the matter so casually. "Helping me out by matching me up with one of your friends? Forget it."

"What could you possibly have against someone trying to fix you up? It could be fun."

He slowly shook his head. "Uh-uh. You're not going to pair me off with anyone when you're unable to do the same for yourself."

"My talents don't extend to me."

"You don't date?"

"Of course I do. Occasionally." She absently picked up a wooden spoon, then set it down again.

Good, he thought. Now *she* was uncomfortable. "So what's happened? Haven't you been able to click with anyone?"

"Click?" She frowned. "People don't click, Matthew. They blend, they spark, but they don't click."

He grinned. "Silly me."

Her frown deepened. "You're making fun of me."

"On the contrary, I'm fascinated. Tell me more, especially about the blending and sparking."

"There's nothing more to tell. And since I'm not a subject of one of your articles—at least I don't think I am—"

"You never can tell. I'm always looking for interesting ideas and new and different angles."

"I'll take that as a warning."

"Why not take it as an invitation?"

"To what?"

"To tell me all about yourself." More comfortable on the offensive, he was beginning to enjoy himself.

"Sorry, but once and for all there's nothing interesting to tell. Would you care for more wine?"

"I've had plenty. And I don't believe you. You've turned into quite a puzzle for me, Samantha, but as it happens, I'm an expert at solving puzzles."

"You sound as if you're taking me on as some sort of project." Inside her a wild kind of excitement collided with a sensible, well-grounded wariness.

"Is there any reason why I shouldn't?"

"Yes, there is. There's no percentage in it,

no payoff. Your readers would be bored out of their minds."

He grinned. "I think you're selling yourself way short, but don't worry about it. I'll decide whether or not there's any percentage."

She felt as if she were standing too close to the edge of a precipice. She knew she should step back, but the excitement increased, keeping her where she was. And the common sense need for wariness was almost forgotten. "Okay, fine, and since you're a self-professed expert on puzzles, you won't need me to tell you anything about myself."

"Not really. It would just make my job easier, but on the other hand if the job is too easy, I lose interest. Besides, I'm great at intuiting."

She clasped her hands together. He was annoying her, *really* annoying her. Grabbing a pair of small scissors, she headed across the kitchen toward a braid of garlic.

Casually he reached out a hand to grasp her arm and swung her down onto his lap. "Don't walk away from me. Please."

She was so astonished to find herself in his lap, she answered without thinking. "The stew needs garlic."

"Anything that smells that good doesn't need one more thing." His voice had turned low and uneven.

"Look, I'm the cook and I think—"

"And I'm your dinner guest. A good hostess tries to please her guest. So, Samantha, how about pleasing me?"

"Matthew . . ." Her voice sounded strange, she thought. Weaker. Softer.

"I bet you would be good at pleasing me," he said roughly. "Just having you on my lap pleases the hell out of me."

His thighs were hard beneath her. The soapy fragrance of his skin along with the undeniable temptation of his blatant masculinity was nearly overpowering her. She tried again, but she couldn't get his name past her throat.

"Yesterday you kept asking me what you could do for me—ask me now. I'd be happy to tell you." He nuzzled her neck and inhaled the perfume of woman unadorned by any scent put together by man. "And speaking of smelling good, I'd rather smell you than a stew any day, and guess which I'd rather eat? . . ."

He didn't have a plan, he hadn't thought out the consequences. He was acting on instinct and need, an instinct and need to discover how she would feel in his arms, how she would taste on his lips. Slowly he nibbled his way up her neck, taking pleasure in each newly discovered spot, its feel, its flavor. He didn't want to stop. But more than that, he couldn't. He continued on across her jaw to her lips, where he took possession.

And a funny, wonderful, totally surprising thing happened. Fragile and supple, she sank against him, all womanly desires and heat. There was no pretense or resistance. Her lips parted, she took his kisses, and she gave and she gave and then she gave some more to him. She surpassed any expectations he might have had, and he was shaken to the core.

She couldn't believe what was happening to her. Heat thundered through her veins, overtaking her completely. She wanted him and in some distant part of her mind she was vaguely shocked. Where had this desire come from? How had it come so quickly, so urgently? Why was the yielding so easy?

Her arms crept around his neck, her fingers slid up into his hair. . . .

The doorbell rang.

At first she didn't recognize the sound— she was too wrapped up in the heat and the sensations—but Matthew did.

Gently, reluctantly he broke off the kiss. With a hand that shook slightly he brushed back her hair from her face. "That's the door."

"Yes," she said, agreeing. "I'll get it."

But she didn't move. She stayed where she was, gazing at him. And she was mesmerized by what she saw. His eyes had gone dark until they were almost black. They were riveting, she thought, eyes a woman could get lost in, eyes that could make a woman forget her better judgment, eyes that could make a woman want to stay close. . . .

"You taste like strawberry wine," he said thickly.

"I haven't had any wine this evening."

"Then I must be tasting myself in you."

The provocative words sent fire shooting straight through her, followed immediately by a cold stream of alarm. The doorbell rang again. *What* had she just allowed to happen? Or maybe the better question was *why* had she just allowed it to happen.

She never lost control, not with a man, not with her life. She prided herself on the fact.

"Do you want to get the door, or shall we just ignore them?"

"No." She had no idea what question she was answering, she reflected vaguely.

Hurriedly she rose and went to the door. Whatever had happened, whatever the reason, she would not let it happen again, of that she was sure. Matthew was a volatile man with a sexuality that was both powerful and explosive. Thank goodness she and Matthew would no longer be alone.

Opening the door, she gratefully greeted Leona and Alfred. "Come in before you get soaked. Sorry it took me so long to answer the bell."

"That's quite all right, my dear," Alfred said, stepping back to allow Leona to enter first. "The porch sheltered us."

"That's right," Leona said, reaching back outside to prop her umbrella against the porch wall. "Besides, it's not as if we'll melt."

Alfred let out a boom of laughter. "I won't, that's for sure, but you might." He turned to address Samantha. "My bride-to-be is one hundred percent pure sugar."

Leona colored prettily. "*Alfred!* Not in front of Samantha!"

He laughed again, and, more relaxed now, Samantha smiled. She loved Alfred's laugh. It was full, robust, and brimming with the joy of life, and it was what had originally drawn her to him as a friend. And he and Leona made a perfect pair in her estimation—Alfred with his beautiful mane of silver hair, elegant and handsome in a nice, though not expensive, suit; and Leona with her brown hair liberally frosted by gray, lovely and young-looking in a rose-colored shirtwaist.

Alfred put his arm around Leona and drew her against his side. "Do you see why I love this woman so much, Samantha? She's still innocent enough to blush."

"Yes, she *is* innocent," Matthew said pointedly, walking into the hallway. "Hello,

Aunt Leona." He extricated her from the other man's hold and bent to kiss her.

She accepted the kiss, but her expression was as severe as she could make it. "I'm still very angry at you, Matthew. In fact by rights I shouldn't even be speaking to you."

"I know," he said with gentle humor. "Maybe you could just use hand signals or write notes."

"I'll think about it. You happen to be very lucky that I love you so much, plus there's the fact that I don't want to ruin Samantha's dinner."

"I am lucky," he agreed.

Relenting, she reached up and lovingly patted his face. Samantha realized Leona had probably been patting his face in just that way since he was a little boy. And his smile was something of a revelation to her. Who would have thought he was capable of such sweetness.

"I'm sorry we were so late," Leona said, "but it was unavoidable. Has Samantha been taking good care of you?"

"Oh, excellent care. Excellent." He glanced at Samantha to see if *she* was still innocent enough to blush. If he'd been a betting man, he would have bet she wasn't. If he'd been a betting man, he would have lost.

She stared back at him, the golden skin of her throat and cheeks faintly tinted with rose.

Like the color of her wine, he thought inconsequentially.

"Why don't you all come into the dining room," she said. "Everything's ready. Alfred, I'm sure you're hungry after working all day."

"That I am."

Matthew spoke up, his tone excruciatingly polite and even. "I can see where greeting people would work up an appetite."

Samantha couldn't detect any sarcasm, but she knew it was there. She was loathe to leave them alone even for a minute, but she had to dart into the kitchen.

Alfred replied in a mild tone. "It's work I enjoy."

Matthew automatically reached over to hold out Leona's chair for her, but Alfred beat him to the punch, making sure she was settled and comfortable before he sat down beside her. Matthew walked around the table and took his seat opposite them. "Since you enjoy working so much, I assume you anticipate continuing to work after you marry my aunt."

His tone was cordial, but Samantha, entering the room with a steaming tureen of stew in her hands, saw the laserlike quality in his eyes and wasn't fooled. Alfred, though, apparently was.

Alfred smiled congenially. "Perhaps for a little while longer, but if you want to know the truth, the only reason I took the job in the first place was because I didn't have anything to do and I was rather lonely. The greeting job got me out of the house and out among people." He turned his head and gazed adoringly at Leona. "But now I have this wonderful lady, and I'd really like to spend as much time with her as possible."

Leona reached out and grasped his hand. "Oh, Alfred, you really are the *sweetest* man."

Between the two lovebirds across from him, sugar fairly coated the air. Viewing the pair cynically, Matthew discovered he'd run out of patience and pressed his point. "But if you quit your job, how will you support my aunt?"

Leona looked shocked. "Matthew, you didn't really believe that Alfred was going to support me on his salary as a greeter, did you?"

"No, I didn't, which is something that has been worrying me. Apparently he thinks he's going to live off of—"

"Here we are," Samantha said, forcing cheerfulness into her voice as she placed the tureen in the center of the table.

"Samantha, darling," Alfred exclaimed, "that smells wonderful."

Matthew didn't like Alfred calling Samantha "darling," as if he were a favorite uncle, and he didn't like the way Alfred kept coming up with excuses to touch Leona. He would feel infinitely better if he could just reach across the table and knock the man's head off, but he knew better. A bull-in-a-china-shop tactic wasn't called for here. The three other people in the room were against him on the matter of the wedding, and Alfred was one smooth customer. So in an attempt to regroup and recall his patience he sat back, drew in a deep, steadying breath, and took a look around him.

They were sitting at a long pine table. Miniature pumpkins, gourds, and small flickering candles served as decoration. A pitcher held honey, its clear golden color visible through the exquisite cut glass. Behind his aunt on the sideboard he could see a bowl of fall tomatoes alongside two homemade pies. One looked like apple—his favorite. Briefly he wondered if she planned to serve ice cream with it. The dishes and cutlery on the table were old and of mixed patterns. The napkins were different colors too. But the variety came together to make a charming picture, a *homey* picture.

A sudden thought struck him, a thought that made him feel better. Maybe a decorator had done Samantha's house. She had said she had grown the vegetables, but perhaps she meant she had *supervised* the garden and employed a gardener. He couldn't imagine her getting her acrylic fingernails dirty, and just about every professional woman he knew in Dallas had acrylic fingernails. He stole a peek at her hands and discovered short, no-nonsense nails bare of polish.

He focused on Samantha as she served each of her guests in turn. In the candlelight her face appeared soft, her skin glowing, much as it might immediately following lovemaking. He took the fantasy a step farther and decided that if indeed it were after lovemaking, she would probably appear soft and glowing all over. At the thought his stomach muscles tightened. She had felt so damned good on his lap, and her mouth beneath his had hardened him to the point of pain.

She filled his bowl and waved toward the baskets of still-warm bread. "Help yourself."

Leona smiled across the table at him. "I'm so glad you took Samantha up on her invitation for dinner, Matthew. I've wanted you to meet Alfred for a long time now."

"You haven't known him that long, Aunt Leona, and I would have been happy to meet Alfred sooner. In fact I've tried several times."

"Yes, I know," Alfred said. "And I owe you an apology. This has been a very busy time for me."

"I thought you said you didn't have anything to do."

"*Before* I met your aunt." He sent Leona a special smile. "But once we started to make wedding plans, there were several things I needed to do, including going to Houston, where my daughter lives, to break the news to her."

"She must have been very happy," Matthew said, and this time the sarcasm came through loud and clear.

"Why don't you try the stew," Samantha said in a voice that sounded like warm honey and drew his gaze to her. "You haven't eaten a thing."

He took a bite, then another. It not only smelled delicious, it *was*. "Who made this?"

Samantha started to reply, but Leona cut her off with a laugh. "Why she did of course. She's an excellent cook, and all the vegetables came from her garden."

He looked at Samantha. "You must have a very good gardener."

She smiled as if, he thought bemusedly, she understood his skepticism.

"I do. It's me. I enjoy gardening, just as I enjoy puttering around the house."

So much for his theory that she hired people to get everything done, he thought, eyeing her smile with suspicion and fascination.

"I never answered you, Matthew," Alfred said. "My daughter couldn't have been happier for me. She knows how lonely I've been since my wife died."

He shifted impatiently. "And my aunt has

been lonely too. I know that, but I'm still very concerned. Aunt Leona, you've worked hard all your life. I want to see you enjoy your old age and—"

"I will, Matthew, when I get to be old." Her eyes twinkled. "Right now I'm enjoying my golden years, and let me tell you that's nowhere near old age."

"Right, well, what I'm trying to prevent is your golden years turning to rust."

Samantha sipped from her water goblet. "What a charming metaphor."

"And apt." He pointed to Alfred. "This man will run straight through her money and leave her when it's gone."

"Thus the rust metaphor," Samantha said to no one in particular, a faint smile on her face.

Matthew was trying to understand why she was smiling, when he heard Alfred say, "Leona, you didn't tell me Matthew was worried that I was after your money."

She frowned uncertainly at her nephew. "I didn't understand that he was. In fact it never occurred to me. I knew he wasn't in favor of the marriage, but I thought it was because he hadn't met you yet and that once he had, all his doubts would disappear."

Matthew reached across the table and closed his hand over hers. "Aunt Leona, I want only what is best for you, and you have to admit that you've had some bad experiences with men in the past."

She withdrew her hand and fixed him with a steel-hard gaze. "Alfred is *not* a mistake, Matthew. He's the best thing that's ever happened to me, and you owe him an apology."

"No, darling, he doesn't. In fact I applaud him for loving you so much that he's looking out for you. It's very commendable."

Leona's face dissolved into a glowing smile. "You're wonderful, Alfred. I don't know what I did to deserve you."

Matthew threw his napkin onto the table in disgust. "Oh, pul-eeze! Give me a *break*. Am I the only one at this table who is seeing straight?"

Samantha leaned toward him and whispered in a conspiratorial tone. "Don't you remember? We've already talked about your vision and the fact that it doesn't extend beyond the end of your nose."

He also leaned forward until their faces were very close. "Such a pretty lady and such a sharp tongue."

"You sound as if the two are usually mutually exclusive."

"In my life they have been."

"That's quite an indictment on the ladies in your life. What a dull time you must have."

"On the contrary, I—"

Leona cleared her throat. "You two can

talk about anything you like as soon as we clear up this misunderstanding about my marriage."

Alfred spread out his hands. "Matthew, my boy, what can I do or say to reassure you?"

Samantha relaxed back in her chair.

With a last look at her he turned to the man across from him. "Confess the truth to my aunt and release her from her engagement to you and this proposed marriage."

"But she knows the truth, and I have no intention of letting her get away from me. That would make me stupid, and I'm not a stupid man."

The two men glared across the table at each other. Leona looked from one to the other, her expression worried.

Samantha lifted her gaze to the ceiling and shook her head. "Alfred, Matthew wants a confession, so give him one. Tell him how much you're worth."

Leona frowned. "Samantha, that would be extremely indelicate."

"Maybe, but it would also provide a quick and tidy solution. Unfortunately your nephew is extremely bullheaded. By the way are you absolutely positive he's your nephew?"

Matthew looked from his aunt to Samantha. "What are you talking about?"

"*Bullheaded.* It means you're—"

"They're talking about how much money I have," Alfred said.

"Darling, you don't have to do this. You're a very private person and—"

He reached over and patted Leona's hand. "I know, but if it will put a smile back on your face, it will be worth it." He looked at Matthew, and when he spoke, his tone was almost apologetic. "You see, I'm worth millions."

"Millions?" Matthew repeated, unsure of the meaning of what he had just heard.

"Yes, actually, quite a few million. In fact hundreds of millions."

Matthew stared at Alfred, dumbfounded. Watching him, Samantha felt a tug of sympathy for him. After all, it was his concern for his aunt that had brought him to this point this evening. She could think of a lot of nephews who wouldn't care or bother.

"Who are you?" he asked. "I mean, I don't recognize the name Alfred Trevarthen."

"That's by my design. I never did like publicity. I founded and for many years ran the Mart, the chain discount department store. A few years ago I sold it for quite a tidy profit."

"The Mart? But that's where you've been working as a greeter."

"I told you. I enjoy the work, and it gave me something to do with my time."

Matthew sat back in his chair and let out a

long breath. Then slowly he turned and looked at Samantha, his hard gaze glittering with ice. "You set me up and let me walk right into that trap."

Immediately all her sympathy for him vanished.

THREE

Without wavering, Samantha returned his gaze. "No one set you up, Matthew."

"You could have told me who Alfred was last night at your office. Nothing would have been easier."

"Would you have believed me? You were so certain Alfred was a fortune hunter, it was really better that you meet him yourself."

"Besides," Leona said, distress apparent in her voice, "it wasn't her place to tell you. She knows what a private person Alfred is. And in the end all she has done is try to help."

"None of this is Samantha's fault, Matthew," Alfred said. "I accept full responsibility. I should have realized how concerned you would be and made the time to see you earlier."

"And she did prepare this lovely dinner,"

Leona said, "and invite us all here so that everything could be straightened out."

Samantha spoke up, amusement heavy in her tone. "You two don't have to defend me. I'm sure Matthew will calm down once he takes the time to think the situation through completely as opposed to reacting in his usual knee-jerk fashion, endearing as I'm sure it is to all of us."

Matthew couldn't take his eyes off Samantha. She might look as if she were made of pure honey and in certain ways be as intoxicating as her homemade wine, but he felt completely justified in his anger. In his mind she had made him look like a fool, and it was a feeling he didn't like. At this very moment he'd love nothing more than to have his hands on her. The urge to strangle her was strong. Even stronger was the urge to kiss her. Damn her for getting to him. Damn him for *letting* her get to him.

"If it will make you feel any better," Alfred was saying to him, "I'll be happy to sign any sort of prenuptial agreement you wish. Under no circumstances would I ever touch a penny of your aunt's money."

Humor glinted in Samantha's eyes as she returned his gaze, humor and something else. Sympathy? Coming from her and at his expense Matthew hated the sight of both. Pulling himself together, he at last looked away from her and toward the couple across from him. "Maybe that would be a good idea, and perhaps Samantha could help us with that." He should get the hell away from her, he thought, but here he was trying to draw her deeper into the situation, and he had no idea why he was doing it.

"I'd be happy to draw up an agreement if that's what everyone wants."

Her lips firmed; Leona shook her head. "That's the most unromantic thing I've ever heard of. There's no way I would sign such a document."

Alfred took her hand. "Now, darling, Matthew is only trying to see that you are protected. It's really a very practical idea."

Leona fixed her intended with an uncharacteristically stern gaze. "Are you afraid I'm after you for your money?"

"No, of course not."

"And I'm not afraid you're after mine. I think that's all we need to know, don't you?"

"Absolutely," Alfred said. "I have enough money for us to enjoy for several lifetimes."

Leona looked back at her nephew. "No prenuptial agreement."

Matthew threw up his hands. "If that's the way you want it. As of this moment I'm officially butting out."

Aware of her duties as hostess, Samantha

smiled. "Wonderful. Now let's all get back to our dinner."

Leona and Alfred began to talk about the wedding, and Samantha did her best to join in. But she found she could give only a small part of her attention to the conversation. Matthew commanded most of her interest. He made an occasional comment, always appropriate and always designed to put his aunt's worries at ease. But she sensed the anger he was taking care to hide and knew his anger was directed at her.

To some extent she could understand. He felt he had been duped and he needed someone to blame. He loved his aunt too much to rain on her parade any more than he already had. Samantha was the next best candidate and she could feel a storm coming on.

Leona hugged Samantha. "Good night, dear. Thank you so much for everything."

"You're entirely welcome. It was my pleasure." She turned to receive a hug from Alfred. "I'll see you two next weekend at the altar."

Leona laughed gaily. "I can't wait. It's going to be a happy day."

Matthew refrained from reminding his aunt that to his knowledge she had said the same thing before her last two weddings. He caught a look from Samantha and had the uncanny feeling she had read his mind. He bent down and kissed his aunt's cheek. "Good night, Aunt Leona."

"Good night, dear. You're not leaving now?"

"No. If it's all right with Samantha, I'd like to stay a little while longer and get to know her better."

Leona beamed. "What a splendid idea. I've been trying to get you two together ever since I met Samantha. I just knew you'd like each other."

The storm was imminent, Samantha thought. Looking at Matthew's expression, she could almost hear the thunder. Fortunately for her she'd never been afraid of storms. "By all means stay."

He shook Alfred's hand. "Good night."

"Good night. I hope we can count on your being there next weekend."

"Of course. I'll be there."

Leona reached up and patted his face. "You've made me very happy, Matthew. Why don't you and Samantha come together?"

And with that suggestion the older couple left. Samantha shut the door after them and turned to face Matthew. "Okay, before you start in on me, would you like something to drink? Perhaps a cup of coffee or a glass of wine?"

"Wine." The moment he said it, he knew he had made a mistake. He should have asked for coffee, something that would keep him clearheaded and straight-thinking. The second mistake he made was in not rescinding his request.

"Fine. I'll meet you in the living room."

He hadn't questioned her request that he tell her what he wanted to drink before he started in on her. She would have been disappointed if he had. She would also have been disappointed if he had left with Leona and Alfred. But then he hadn't disappointed her once since she had met him. She always knew where he was coming from. And she realized she was looking forward to their upcoming conversation.

Carrying a tray bearing two glasses of wine, she walked into the living room and discovered he had added fresh logs to the fire. She handed him his glass and sat down at the opposite end of the couch from him, facing him. "Well?"

"Well what?"

"I'm waiting. I know you're angry with me."

He looked down at the golden-rose color of the wine in his glass and remembered its delicate and faintly sweet taste. The wine held the potential for intoxication, just as she did. He had asked for the wine, he realized, simply because he had wanted to hold it, look at it, smell it, when in reality it was *her* he wanted to look at, hold, smell. . . . The golden-rose liquid quivered. His hand was trembling. Damn.

Without taking so much as a sip he carefully set the glass down. "If you want to know the truth, I'm mad as hell at you."

"Because I'm the easiest target."

He smiled slightly. "There's nothing easy about you, Samantha."

"You know what I mean."

"Yeah, okay, even a *hint* of who Alfred was would have helped me out."

"I doubt it. You had made up your mind."

"Minds can be changed."

"From what I've seen, I don't think yours can be changed easily. Are you always so single-minded about going after answers to issues you see as a problem?"

"Always, Samantha. Always."

His eyes had narrowed on her, his voice had lowered, and she had the oddest feeling the problem he had in mind was her. She reached for a throw pillow and placed it in the corner of the sofa behind her back, trying to get more comfortable. "Okay, so are you satisfied about Alfred?"

"Pretty much. The time for any real cynicism is obviously past."

She gazed at him curiously. "Is trusting

even *possible* with you? Can you *not* be cynical?"

Instead of giving her a quick, flippant answer, he surprised himself by giving some thought to her question. "I'm sure there must be some things I'm trusting about, but at the moment I can't think of one. As for Alfred I'll verify his story, but I'm just about certain he told the truth."

"Just about certain? You still have a doubt?"

"I simply think it would be wise to check him out, and now that I understand who he is, it will be easy because I'll know where to look. But there's no doubting the two of them are in love. I hope it will last, but if it doesn't, Aunt Leona won't be any poorer for the experience."

Samantha stared at him. "I don't think I've ever met anyone more cynical and suspicious than you."

"Oh, come now, Samantha. Not even you?"

"Me?"

"I would think as a divorce lawyer you'd see people at their worst."

"I certainly see them at their most unhappy, but I won't take a divorce case unless I honestly think the marriage was a mistake in the first place and the two will be better off without each other. And even then I *strongly* suggest they both attend counseling so they won't make the same mistake again."

"And you accused *me* of playing God?" He moved down the couch toward her, and when he stopped, his hitched-up knee rested on a part of her dress, pinning her to the spot. Then he reached out and lightly touched a russet-colored strand streaked with gold that lay over her shoulder.

She went still. "Don't."

He pulled his hand away, but he slid his arm along the top of the couch until his fingers were a movement away from her hair, her neck, her face. He cocked his head to the side and looked at her. "Okay, then, tell me why you think you, who have never been married and can't even match yourself up with anyone, are qualified to make those kinds of judgments about a couple."

She took a sip of her wine. It was the first sip she had had this evening, but she felt as unsteady as if she'd had ten full glasses. "I'm not playing God. I simply have good instincts about those sorts of things and I trust them."

"You're saying your instincts are your qualifications?"

"What else does anyone have? Don't you have certain instincts when it comes to following leads in a story?"

"Yeah, I do, but I don't make vast, sweeping judgments about people without a lot of hard evidence."

"I don't either. I ask questions, I listen." She twisted to set the glass on the end table.

"And you don't think people lie to you?"

"If they lie to me, I eventually find out, but until I do, I go on the premise that they're telling me the truth, which I gather is the exact opposite of what you do."

His fingers shifted to her hair. It felt like silk and smelled like everything good the earth had ever made, which was how she smelled too. Fresh, natural, sweet. "You're right. I always go on the premise that people are lying to me." She was a lie. She had to be.

She sensed rather than felt his touch on her hair. Slowly excitement seeped into her. The last time they had been this close, he had kissed her, and she had turned into fire. Even now heat was winding through the pit of her stomach. She swallowed and discovered the muscles of her throat had tightened. "And you don't trust me."

He shifted his fingers to her face and lightly caressed her cheek. "Not even a little bit."

His breath fanned her face. His nearness was swamping her senses. She could have moved, she should have moved. She didn't. "Why? What have I done to you?"

"That's a damn good question." His fingers skimmed to her lips, his gaze followed. With the pad of his fingers he explored the soft fullness, outlining the shape, learning the texture. With each moment that passed, his pulse became quicker and quicker; with each breath he drew, his body grew harder and harder. "Damn good question," he said again, "but sweetheart, you've definitely done something to me."

He was running out of oxygen, and the room was filled with air; he was drowning and there was no water in sight. He needed help in the worst way, but he knew he wasn't going to get it. In fact he didn't want it. He lowered his head and replaced his fingers with his mouth. And her sweet taste of honey and wine undid him.

Once again she gave no resistance. Once again she turned into fire. Their first kiss had come as a surprise to her, but somehow she had known this kiss would happen. In fact, she realized, she had anticipated it, waited for it. It was why she hadn't moved.

Slowly she leaned back against the arm of the couch, and with a growl he followed her, pressing his big body against hers. She changed positions to better take his weight, then arched against him. She was hungry, she was needy, she was without thought. His mouth made demands on hers that she met without question. She'd known him only a little more than twenty-four hours and she shouldn't be this pliable in his arms, this desperate. He didn't trust her, and she didn't know if she trusted him, but at this moment it didn't seem to matter.

What was between them, what was happening, wasn't the real thing where love drove everything from heart to body. No, only the body was involved in this, but it didn't matter. What was happening felt good, and there would be no harm done. She would see that there wasn't.

He tightened his hold on her and shifted them both until they were lying on the couch with him half on top of her. He needed the contact. His body was hurting for her, his heart was pounding. He felt like a teenager with all his appetites and hormones running out of control. He craved her and he wasn't sure he could stop until he had had all of her.

He slipped his hand beneath her skirt and smoothed his fingers up her thigh. She made a soft sound, but he couldn't tell whether it was one of approval or displeasure.

"What?" he asked roughly, sliding his hand higher. "Tell me what you want."

"Stop."

"Stop what? Kissing you?"

"No."

"Stop touching you? I'm not sure I can." The softness of her skin was indescribable and went to his head as surely as her wine had. His fingers brushed against the elastic of her panties.

"Don't . . . go any farther." Pain laced her tone. She could barely get the words out. It was one of the hardest things she'd ever had to ask, because quite simply she wanted him and knew she shouldn't.

With his mouth on hers he groaned, and his fingers stilled just beneath the elastic. He could feel her heat, and if he had continued only a little farther, he would have been able to feel her moistness. "Why? Tell me why."

"Because," she whispered with her lips pressed to his, "we'll regret it if you continue."

"I won't." Certain he was going to come apart if he didn't have her, he thrust his tongue deep into her mouth. His need for her was devastating him.

His kiss was an assault, bombarding her with pleasure and desire. Unconsciously she moved her hips, and when she did, his finger slipped into her. Had she done it? Had he? It didn't matter. His touch felt so good. . . .

With a moan she gripped his shoulders, using all her strength, trying desperately to hold on to reality. But she was lost. Her only hope was him.

"Matthew . . ."

Uttering a violent curse, he pulled himself

up and off her and propelled himself across the room to the fireplace, where he stared blindly down at the fire. He wouldn't be able to look at her without going back to her, and once he had gone back to her, he wouldn't be able to stop himself from taking her. The heat licked against his lower body, but it was nothing compared with the heat that gripped his insides.

"Matthew . . ."

His jaw clenched. "Sit up, Samantha."

She couldn't remember a time when she had been as embarrassed as she was now. And to make matters worse, her body still throbbed and ached for him. Struggling, awkward, she did as he said, straightening her clothes, running shaky fingers through her hair, doing her best to compose herself. After a minute she said, "I'm sorry, Matthew. This is all my fault."

"Not entirely."

"Yes, yes, it is. I—"

"Shut up, Samantha." He turned and looked at her. "Don't say any more."

"Maybe you're right. Enough has been said, done. . . . But I'd like to say one more thing. I'd like to ask you to leave."

"Yeah, sure, right. I'll leave just as soon as you tell me what in the hell just happened."

"I can't. I don't know. But it was definitely

a mistake, and it's good that we stopped before things got out of hand."

"Good? *Good*, Samantha? Then why do I feel so damned bad?"

She passed a hand over her face. "Just go, Matthew."

"Is that how you handle things you can't explain? You just make them go away?"

"Sometimes it's the best way."

"Well, it's not my way. I try to figure out things I can't explain. And you, Samantha, are damned hard to explain."

"That sounds like a warning."

"Take it any way you like."

FOUR

Matthew grimaced at the sight of the recently refilled cup of coffee in front of him. He had lost count of how many cups he had drunk, but his mouth tasted like the inside of an athletic shoe and his nerves were sparking like live electric wires.

It was around eleven o'clock at night and he had spent the last few hours in a dive of a café on the outskirts of downtown Dallas waiting for Joe Gates to show. The café featured peeling Formica tables and cracked vinyl booths and a tired waitress who had begun to give him irritated looks.

If he thought for one moment that Gates was leading him on, he would have been out of the coffee shop long ago. But he had too many years' experience to doubt the man's sincere wish to tell him what he knew about the well-known judge Richard Barnett. Gates had the very best reason there was: His neck was on the block.

And so he would wait a little while longer.

As it often had during the day and evening —too often, actually—his thoughts drifted back to Samantha and the night before. He had long ago lost his ability to be shocked by anyone, man or woman. But Samantha definitely intrigued him. And nettled him. And continued to catch him off guard.

Earlier in the day he had received a phone call from a friend of Samantha's, a Rosalyn Davies. Rosalyn had told him that Samantha had given her his phone number and suggested that the two of them might get along famously. He had mustered a combination of finesse and manners and had politely rebuffed the woman, then he had promised himself that whatever game Samantha was playing, she wouldn't win.

Wearily he rubbed his face and glanced at his watch. Gates wasn't going to show tonight, but he wasn't discouraged. Tomorrow was another day, and he was used to long waits and dead ends. It was all part of the job.

Rising, he dropped an extra-generous tip on the table and walked out into the night.

At her home Samantha lay propped up in bed amid a myriad of plump pillows and leafed through her address book. Rosalyn had called her and told her that Matthew had turned her down. After consoling her friend with the promise that she'd keep an eye out for someone else for her, she had begun racking her brains over another friend Matthew might like. The problem was she seemed to find something wrong with all of them, and she'd been back and forth through her address book at least a dozen times.

Stopping on one page near the back, she thoughtfully frowned down at a name. Maggie Webster. Of course—*Maggie*. Why hadn't she considered her before? She was bright, fun, and most of all adaptable. She would be ideal for Matthew.

But she hesitated. *Why was she doing this*, trying to match Matthew up with the perfect woman for him?

Was she doing it for Leona? Sure. Leona had told her she thought Matthew would be much happier when he finally settled down with just the right woman. He worked too hard, Leona had said with a worried expression. It would be good if she could relieve Leona's worry about her nephew. Wouldn't it?

Was she doing this for Maggie? Again, yes. Like all her single friends, Maggie was constantly looking for Mr. Right, not that she had

any trouble getting dates. Maggie was spectac-
ular-looking. Of course Maggie smoked, and
Matthew didn't. But then again Maggie had
been vowing to stop. . . .

Was she doing this for Matthew? Forget it.
On his longest day he wouldn't be apprecia-
tive of her efforts.

A small smile slowly curved her lips. "Oh,
well, why not?" And she reached for the
phone.

The golden November sunlight did its
best to warm the clear, crisp day, but a stiff
breeze kept the air cool and the leaves cart-
wheeling and skimming along the grass and
sidewalks. Matthew took the courthouse steps
two at a time and pushed open the door.

A call from a panicky Joe Gates had awakened him. He hadn't been able to show up last
night, Gates had said, because his boss had
been too suspicious. But he had to see Matthew *today*. For sure he'd be at a certain park
at noon.

Matthew had spent a couple of hours at
the office putting the final touches on another
assignment, then decided he had a little time
to see Samantha.

He found her in court, exactly where her
secretary, the estimable Barbara, had said she
would be. He slipped into a seat at the back of

the courtroom, a seat that gave him an excellent view of her. After watching her for a few moments, he realized he was looking at the woman he had met that first day.

Cool, competent, never raising her voice or exposing ruffled emotions, she was wearing a pumpkin-colored, tailored suit with matching suede, low-heeled shoes. The gold-and-leather watch gleamed on her wrist. And her hair—the same glorious silky stuff he had sunk his fingers into two nights earlier—was once again smoothed into a perfect, no-nonsense twist.

Where had the Samantha of the spices, honey, and vanilla gone? The Samantha who wore a fragile, floating dress and ballet slippers and turned to fire in his arms?

Here in the courtroom she was every inch the lawyer intent on her client's best interest, in this case a sad, but stoic-looking man in his early forties who sat quietly but with obvious confidence in her. On the other side of the courtroom a woman sat, equally sad but also resolved. The man's wife, Matthew surmised. How could Samantha do this? he wondered, day in and day out, exposing herself to the unhappiness and decay of other people's lives?

Then again he did exactly the same thing. But he did it for the truth. Why did she do it?

Samantha had known the moment Matthew had entered the courtroom, although she hadn't done much more than throw a surreptitious glance his way. But she had *felt* his presence the way someone might feel heat against his or her skin. Excitement had slipped into her bloodstream; all her senses had become alert. He was like a magnetic force to which some inner compass in her responded, making it hard for her not to turn toward him.

But she forced her concentration back to the case at hand and finished her business before the court. Afterward she had a brief talk with her client, ensuring to her satisfaction that he would be all right. And then and only then did she allow herself to turn toward Matthew.

Her first impression was that he was lounging comfortably, but that was impossible. No one could actually be comfortable on the courtroom's wooden, utilitarian benches. But if she could rule out comfortable in her mind, she couldn't rule out that he certainly appeared at ease and relaxed, leaning back, his arms spread along the top of the bench on either side of him, his legs crossed with one ankle resting atop the opposite knee.

However, his deep-blue gaze was not relaxed; he was staring at her with an unsettling concentration. A glance around her informed her that the courtroom was quickly clearing. Soon there would be only the two of them left. Hurriedly she gathered her papers to-

Fayrene Preston
74

gether and inserted them into her briefcase, then strolled to where he was seated.

He rose as she approached. "Good job. Another marriage shredded. Another few dollars earned."

Because there was no malice behind his words, she ignored his sarcasm. He was obviously annoyed with her today, but she had the certain feeling it wasn't because of her profession. "Hello, Matthew. What are you doing here?"

He casually slipped his hands into his trouser pockets. "Checking out divorce lawyers. At the rate you're going, I may need one."

"Me?"

"Yesterday I got a call from your friend Rosalyn."

"Yes, I know. She said you were very firm but polite. Thank you for that, being polite, I mean."

"It wasn't her fault."

Her chin came up. "I was only trying to help you, Matthew."

"Help, Samantha? What have I done or said to lead you to believe that I need help?"

"Nothing," she admitted. "But Leona has mentioned a time or two that she'd like to see you find the right woman and settle down."

"Once my aunt is married, she'll have a lot less time to worry about me, which, I might add, will be to the greater good of all involved. Besides, being single is in no way, shape, or form cause for concern. Look at you—you're single—and apparently you aren't out beating the bushes for a mate for yourself, are you?"

"No. Absolutely not." She glanced at her watch, more an idle habit than a necessity at this point in her day's schedule.

"You're happy, aren't you?"

Her head jerked up. "Of course I am."

"Then maybe you can give me the same grace you give yourself on this subject and butt the hell out of my personal life."

"Absolutely, if that's what you'd like. But you would have liked Rosalyn. She's very nice."

"She sounded as if she was. Just like your friend Maggie did this morning."

Her eyes widened slightly. "Maggie called you?"

"Wasn't that what you wanted her to do?"

"Yes, of course. It's just that I wasn't certain she'd call so soon."

"Why not? Both of your friends sounded very eager. You must have given me quite a buildup."

Feeling awkward and defensive, she shrugged. "Not really."

"Uh-huh."

Her beeper went off. Seizing the distraction, she took her time studying the number.

He stepped closer to her. "Well, let me tell you something, Samantha, just in case this point hasn't occurred to you. It's damned unsettling to have a woman with whom I came so close to making love try her dead-level best to dump me on first one, then another of her friends."

Dozens of responses leaped to her mind, but she focused on the most important one. "We *didn't* nearly make love."

"Oh, yeah? Funny. I could have sworn that was you."

"You know what I mean—"

He reached for her, wound his long fingers around her upper arms, and pulled her to him. "Let's just see. . . ."

His mouth came down on hers in one very hard, very thorough kiss that involved every one of her senses. She was so surprised, it didn't occur to her to struggle. They were in a public place. Nothing would happen. Nothing, but a shattering of resolve and composure. . . .

Nothing and everything.

Her body softened, her insides heated, hunger flared. She'd never known a man's kiss like Matthew's, she thought vaguely. She'd never known a man like Matthew. With him there was instant surrender, no matter where and no matter what. With him there was instant desire—powerful, needy desire that threatened boundaries and endangered absolutes.

Slowly she became aware that he was breaking off the kiss. And she heard his voice, raspy and gruff, very near her ear.

"I was right. The woman I was with night before last definitely tasted like you do. And" —he bent his head once more, this time to place his lips against the side of her neck— "she certainly smelled like you do. Honey, vanilla . . . What in the hell kind of perfume do you wear, anyway? You're the most intoxicating woman I've ever met."

She dug for strength and wrested away from him. With a shaking hand she touched her lips. They were hot, throbbing. Reaching up, she tried to smooth her hair, then belatedly decided it was futile. Her hand dropped back to her side. "What did you tell her?"

"Who?" His beeper hooked to his belt went off, but he merely pressed the button to stop the sound and kept his darker-than-usual-blue eyes fixed on her lips.

"Maggie. What did you tell her?"

His gaze lifted to her face. A delicate pink rose tinted the pale gold skin of her cheeks and offered an interesting contrast to the color of her pumpkin suit. "I told her I'd call her back."

Her stomach hurt, she realized. Maybe she

was hungry. Or maybe she had a case of indigestion. "You did?"

"Sure. Isn't that what you wanted?" At her slight nod he went on. "As I said, she sounded nice . . . and interesting."

"She is. I wouldn't have given her your number if I hadn't thought you'd like her." She looked around for her briefcase, which had dropped to the floor beside her sometime during the kiss. She picked it up, then looked back at him, troubled, confused, hurting. "Well . . ."

He took the initiative. "I'll see you later."

"Right. Later."

He watched her as she walked out of the courtroom. When he could no longer see her, he smiled. And then and only then did he check his beeper for the number.

Matthew found Joe Gates sitting at a picnic table, feeding peanuts to an attentive band of squirrels. Appearing to be in his early thirties, Gates was a slim, well-dressed man and held an up-and-coming position with a highly organized, highly successful Texas criminal cartel.

Matthew dropped down beside him, his back to the table. "Glad you finally made it."

"Yeah, sorry about last night, but it couldn't be helped. I've got to be careful."

"I understand."

"Listen, are you going to be able to help me?"

Matthew calmly returned the man's nervous gaze. "I'm hoping we're going to be able to help each other, but it depends on what you've got."

"Like I told you, it's about Judge Richard Barnett and Spencer Tate."

Matthew nodded. Tate was one of the cartel's top lieutenants. Gage worked for Tate. "As I understand it, Tate is up on delivery and manufacture of controlled substances, plus engaging in organized criminal activity."

"Right." He tossed another handful of peanuts to the squirrels. "That's public knowledge, but what isn't is that pressure is being applied to Barnett to dismiss the case or rule against."

"Pressure? You mean he's being blackmailed?"

"Yes. Several months ago the judge had a brief but very hot affair with a woman who works at the courthouse."

"Barnett? Well, well, imagine that." Matthew wasn't particularly surprised, but he was definitely interested. Barnett's reputation was that of an upstanding family man who stood for truth, justice, and the American way. Occasionally the society section of the paper would run a picture of the judge at some civic

function or another, and he always appeared
with his family, a good-looking group if Matthew remembered correctly. A wife, two boys,
and a girl. Or was it two girls and a boy? "Was
it a setup?"

"No. That's the great thing about it from
the organization's viewpoint. Ever since Barnett was assigned to the case, they've been
dogging the judge's trail, trying to pick up
something on him they could use. There was
nothing for a while, and then they got lucky."

"Who is she?"

"I don't have a name. All I know is that
she's someone who works at the courthouse
and is a real hot number. Apparently she's
someone he's known for a while, and the
temptation finally got too great. The judge
caved."

"You don't have anything else on her? A
description or what department she works
in?"

"No."

"What about *which* courthouse? Criminal
or civil?"

He shook his head. "No. I've heard her
described in only the most general terms. You
know, great-looking with legs to write home
about and autumn-colored hair."

Something inside Matthew went cold.
"Autumn-colored hair?"

"Yeah, I don't know, that's just what I was told. Listen, is this enough?"

"Not even close. So far all you've given me is hearsay. I need hard facts with resources I can quote. But I'm definitely interested. I'll have to nose around the courthouse and see what I can pick up. In the meantime see what other information you can get for me."

"But it's the truth, and if it goes down like the organization thinks, Barnett is going to throw the case, and Tate is going to walk. You can't tell me that's not a big story."

"Oh, it's big, okay. Big for you, too, huh?"

Gage looked away. "Tate's been preoccupied lately, trying to find a way to get himself off. But if he gets a walk on this, he's going to turn his attention back to his own backyard."

"Which is exactly where you are."

"Right." Gage's lips flattened grimly. "I did something really stupid with some funds, thinking I could settle it up later. Unfortunately later has turned into *much* later, and now I don't see a way to fix it. If Tate discovers what I've done, the authorities will find me at the bottom of Lake Worth with my feet in cement."

"Clichéd but effective."

"Yeah."

Matthew rose. "Stay in touch and do what you can to find out more details about the woman. If I could get her corroboration, it would make the story."

A woman who worked at the courthouse with legs to write home about and autumn-colored hair.

The description kept repeating in Matthew's mind all afternoon. Just below the surface of his skin uneasiness prickled and anger simmered.

The description fit Samantha perfectly. But it must also fit a dozen other women. And Samantha had never said or done anything that would make him think she would have an affair with a married man.

Except . . .

She had an extraordinary ability to compartmentalize her life. In the little time he had known her, he had seen two distinct sides of her. Which one was real? Were there more than two sides? He intended to find out.

He had contacts at both the courthouses and he spent the afternoon pursuing them. Getting information was tricky business. He had to convey what he wanted to know without letting on *why* he wanted to know or seeming too eager. He had had years of experience doing it, but the string he was following on this story bothered him. Consequently later in the day when he looked back on his time at the courthouse, he could recall half a dozen times he had been totally ineffective. He put in a few more hours at the office, then called it a day. Fighting the urge to call Samantha, he went to bed early and was rewarded by poor sleep.

He felt like a bear when he awoke the next morning, surly and distinctly out of sorts. And he immediately decided to resolve the matter once and for all. He called Samantha and caught her at home.

"Good morning," he said. "Sleep well?"

"I always sleep well."

"Figures," he muttered.

"What?"

"Nothing. Listen I'm trying to track something down at the courthouse and I was wondering if you could help me."

"In what way?"

Wariness and reserve underscored her question, and he supposed he couldn't blame her. He had deliberately thrown her a couple of curves yesterday. He had kissed her, then told her he was going to call her friend. Kissing her had been a compulsion he couldn't control. Telling her he was going to call her friend had been an attempt to serve her a portion of her own medicine. He had figured if she had him off balance, he should return the favor. But in the end, when he was left alone to remember the kiss, he hadn't been able to decide which of them had won the encounter.

"Do you know Judge Richard Barnett?"

His question was met by silence. Finally she asked, "Why?"

"I told you. I'm just trying to run a couple of leads down."

"About what?"

"Samantha, do you or don't you know the judge?"

"We work in different courthouses. Generally speaking, he sits on criminal cases. Is there anything else?"

"Generally speaking? You mean he may have overseen other types of cases before? Civil, for instance?"

"It happens."

"So do you know him or not?"

"Everyone knows of the judge."

"But I'm not asking about everyone. I'm asking about you."

"And I told you. What's all this about, anyway?"

"Just something I'm trying to track down."

Dammit, she stumped him. Not only wasn't she answering his questions, he couldn't find the conviction to keep pursuing the subject. "I guess I can assume you're going to the wedding this weekend."

"I think I already told you I was."

"You'll have to forgive me, Samantha. I've been forgetting a lot of things lately."

Samantha's hand tightened on the receiver. He hadn't forgotten a thing. "Have
you called Maggie yet?"

"No, I haven't had time."

"I'm sure she'd love to hear from you."

"And I'm quite sure it's nothing for you to
worry about. Talk to you later."

"Yeah, good-bye." She hung up the receiver but continued staring down at the
phone as if the act could conjure Matthew
back to her, his voice, his tone, and give her a
clue as to what that phone call had really been
about.

Something was wrong. Why had he asked
her about Richard? And why had she felt the
need to equivocate as she had?

Instinct, pure and simple.

Matthew might find it hard to believe, but
she admired and respected his journalistic
abilities to such an extent that she would never
want anyone important to her to be his target.

With a glance at the time, she picked up
the phone and dialed Judge Richard Barnett's
office.

FIVE

Late Friday night several evenings later Matthew pulled his car to a stop in front of Samantha's house. A couple of the windows glowed with light. He could just make out a pale plume of smoke coming from the chimney, a lighter gray against the darker color of the sky. She must be home. Whether she was alone or not was a different matter, but he didn't really care. Not in the mood he was in.

It was the damnedest thing. He felt as if he were bursting with restless energy, restless *uncomfortable* energy. It made him want to *do* something, mainly about Samantha.

Right now he wanted nothing more than to barge into her home and take it apart piece by piece for clues as to who she really was and what she was all about. But he knew he still wouldn't be satisfied, not until he had taken *her* apart, part by luscious part of her body, inch by sweet inch of her skin. She was preying on his mind, knotting up his system, making him antsy and impatient.

And this damned Barnett story. He was getting nowhere, going down more dead ends than usual. He was ready to walk away from it —an unusual attitude for him. Tomorrow he supposed he would try again. Maybe he would set up a loose surveillance on the judge. He'd think about it later. But for tonight he was going to concentrate on Samantha.

He bounded up the steps and rang the bell. When she opened the door, he saw her backlighted by the hall light, so beautiful, so desirable. Her russet-colored hair lay in loose, shining disorder around her shoulders, as if every now and then during the evening she had absently run her hands through it. She glowed like a flame, her skin golden and free of any makeup. Her eyes, however, showed confusion and wariness.

"Matthew? What are you doing here?"

"Are you alone?"

"Yes. Why?"

"May I come in?"

"Is anything wrong? Has something happened to Leona or Alfred?"

"No, no, nothing like that. I'd like to talk to you."

"Very well, come in."

She walked ahead of him, leading him down the hall and into the living room. She was wearing a lounging gown that fell in a straight line without buttons or zippers to her bare feet. As she walked, the thin, gold, velvet material clung and outlined her slim body. His imagination went into overdrive, and he wondered if she wore anything beneath it.

Just looking at her made him feel as if he had been hit with a club—breathless, stunned, his adrenaline rushing out of control. Damn!

And the house, it smelled sweet, clean, spicy, just as it had the other night. A fire crackled in the fireplace. Quiet, intimate music wafted softly on the air. A cream-colored afghan with multicolored ribbons woven through the weave of the crochet work was thrown across the end of the sofa. Nearby a book lay open. The room looked warm and relaxing, yet he had never felt more tense in his life.

He turned and found Samantha watching him. "Were you reading?"

She nodded. "It's a book on gardening. Sit down. Can I get you something to drink?"

"No, nothing."

If he'd gone to her office and found her reading, he would have bet money she would have been reading a legal-type thriller or perhaps a time-management self-help book. But in her home he wasn't surprised to find her reading about gardening.

Samantha considered him. The navy shirt he wore was open at the neck, the jeans well worn, but the dark-chocolate-brown sports jacket was expensive and elegantly tailored. Matthew's presence was like a natural disturbance, putting an end to the peace of her evening. She wouldn't have been surprised to hear thunderstorms brewing outside, because inside, the atmosphere had changed. It was now charged, electric.

She picked up the afghan, then after a moment's thought held it against her and dropped into the corner of the sofa opposite from him.

He eyed her consideringly as he sat. "That's interesting. I've never seen anyone try to use something as soft and flimsy as an afghan for protection."

She glanced down at the bundle in her arms, but she didn't move to put it aside. "Why would I need protection?"

"You tell me."

With a sigh she brushed her hair back from her face. "Let's cut out the games tonight, Matthew. *You* came here to see *me*— remember? You said you wanted to talk to me. Okay, what about?"

He should have been prepared for the question, but he wasn't. When he'd headed in this direction tonight, he'd only been aware of the need to see her once again, to be with her. Now he was here, almost within touching distance of her, and she looked more sensually feminine than anyone he'd ever seen. And amazingly more innocent. With her he sometimes felt as if he had stepped into an alternate universe woven of enchantment. And he wasn't sure he believed any of it. "I'd like to get to know you better."

"Why?"

"Why?" he repeated, hard pressed to keep the sharpness from his tone, a sharpness that revealed the ragged state of his nerves. "Because mere days ago I didn't know you, and now you've become a part of my life."

"Not really."

"Oh, you're *way* too modest, Samantha. You were instrumental in introducing my aunt —someone very important to me—to the man she's going to marry. And now you're trying to find someone to match me up with."

"I've stopped."

His brows shot up. "Since when?"

"Since you said you were going to call Maggie."

"So you consider your job with me done?"

"It wasn't a job, and I'm sorry if you feel I've been meddling."

"Are you? And are you *really* going to stop trying to fix me up with your friends?"

"Yes, because I've found the perfect person for you. Maggie's the best. You'll see."

"Yeah, I'll see. And I hope *you'll* see—or at least understand—why I'm mildly curious about the person who's having such a major influence on my life."

"I don't see that anything I've done has influenced you one way or the other, so, no, I don't understand. And I also don't understand why now, tonight? It's late."

"I wasn't doing anything else important tonight. Were you?"

"Look, Matthew, I don't mean to be ungracious, but I'm tired and I was relaxing a little before I called it a night."

"Do you want me to leave?"

Taking her time, she rearranged the afghan neatly against her. His sudden appearance on her doorstep had thrown her. He looked too alert, too much like someone who could set her on fire with his kisses, too much like someone she'd been trying to forget. "Why do I feel as if I've suddenly become the focus of one of your investigations?"

"I don't know, but I will say one thing. If you *were* the focus of one of my investigations, you'd be a damned fascinating one. I've never known anyone quite like you."

"Somehow I don't think that's a compliment."

"Believe me it is."

He'd asked if she wanted him to leave, but she didn't entertain the idea even for a moment. For one thing it would be cowardly of her. For another she knew the burning heat of his intensity, and still she found she couldn't resist dancing near the flame. "Okay, Matthew, what do you want to know?"

"Well, for instance, let's start with your profession."

"Is this going to be twenty questions?" she asked guardedly.

"Maybe forty."

Her lips quirked. "I feel as though I'm going to be at a definite disadvantage. Asking questions is your profession."

"And if I didn't know better, I'd say that dodging questions was yours."

She sighed with resignation. "What's your question?"

"Why did you decide to become a divorce lawyer?"

"That's easy. I always wanted to be a lawyer. My dad was one."

"A divorce lawyer?"

"No. He was a corporate lawyer, but having businesses rather than people as clients never appealed to me."

It was a reasonable explanation. He recalled her courtroom demeanor while studying her as she was now. She presented fascinating contrasts, but all he wanted to know was which was the real Samantha. "You say your dad *was*? Is he retired?"

"Deceased. About eight years ago."

"That would have been before you graduated law school."

"That's right."

"And your mom?"

"She's remarried to a very nice man."

"Let me guess—you introduced them."

"No. They found each other on their own."

"What happened? Were you on vacation or something?"

She stared at him.

"Sorry. I couldn't resist."

"Try a little harder next time."

"I'll see what I can do."

He grinned, and watching him, she knew that next time his sarcasm would be just as quick and just as sharp.

"So you chose to be a divorce lawyer because you wanted to work with people?"

A log fell in the fireplace, sending sparks shooting up toward the flue. Her gaze idly followed them, a needed, brief respite from gazing into Matthew's deep-blue eyes. "You know, Matthew, life very rarely offers clearcut paths for people to follow. Usually a person goes down one path for a while, loses interest or gets diverted, and then chooses another path. Sometimes a person can follow a great many paths before he or she finds the right one. Didn't you?"

"Not really. I always knew I wanted to look for the real story, the truth that lay beneath the false surface."

"But all surfaces aren't false."

The firelight was casting a glow over her hair, and he was having a hard time telling the difference between the velvet texture of what she wore and the velvet texture of her skin. False surfaces could be damnably enticing. "No, but instinct tells me which are. When I look at something—or someone—and it seems too good to be true, it usually is. Or if I look at something or someone and I'm troubled or puzzled, then I know there's more to the situation than I'm seeing."

"I respect that ability, Matthew."

"You do?"

She smiled at his surprise. "Yes, I do, but having said that, I also have to say that journalists as a whole can let their instincts get out of control. They go after stories that are really no one's business but the people involved and they end up hurting people who don't deserve to be hurt."

"Who exactly are we talking about here?" he asked softly.

"Journalists."

"*I'm* a journalist."

"I've already said that I'm talking about your profession as a whole."

"And so I shouldn't take any of this personally?"

"Only if you think it fits."

"I guess we could sit here all night and argue about what fits and what doesn't fit. In fact it seems you and I can argue about just about any subject."

"What's bothering you, Matthew?"

"You, Samantha. *You.*"

He didn't move, but he spoke with such intimacy and softness, she felt as if he had touched her. Heat glided over her skin. "Why in the world would I bother you?"

The question pricked at his nerves, the answer even more so. "I don't know. I'm not sure."

"That's hard to believe. You seem so sure about everything else."

His eyes narrowed at her retort. "Okay, then, I know at least part of *why*. You bother me because there are two distinct sides to you, and I don't know which one, if either, to trust."

Why was it important to him to trust her? It was an obvious question, but the answer, she reflected, might bring complications she wasn't ready to deal with. "So let me get this straight—you think I might be untrustworthy, part of me or all of me, one side or another, whatever the *side* thing means." She shook her head in bewilderment. "What makes you think I care what you think?"

He smiled, baring his teeth. "Why don't you just take it as a compliment that I'm even putting in the effort to try to figure you out."

"Forgive me for saying this, but you give the strangest compliments of any man I've ever known."

"And you've known a lot of men? In the biblical sense?"

"I think you just veered *way* off the subject."

"I'm flexible."

"I'm not, and it's *none* of your business, Matthew."

He shrugged. "Okay, *Men You Have Known* is off-limits as a subject. For now. What about getting back to your profession? Is that a safe enough subject for you?"

She let out a long breath. She had to remember that this man was an expert at eliciting responses from people, and she needed to do a better job of not letting him get to her. "My profession—okay? I chose to be a divorce attorney because I felt I could help people. A divorce is one of the most difficult things that can happen, whether it's wanted or not. In effect, it's a severing of a life two people have created together. They're cutting themselves off from the person they once thought they loved more than anyone else in the world. I *hate* the idea of divorce, but if it has to be done, I can do it with the least trauma to all concerned."

"But how can you enjoy doing something you hate?"

"I concentrate on repairing lives rather than on tearing them apart. When a miserable or impossible situation ends, a new, better life can begin."

"Yeah, but—"

"I'm not saying it's easy. It's not. But it's what I do, I do it well, and there is the reward of making things better."

He stared at her. "So you expose yourself to other people's heartache because you feel you can help."

"That's right."

Her reason wasn't so very far removed from his reason, he thought. He sought truth, and truth always helped people. "And in your off time you put people together whom you feel are right for each other and you come home to this house." He was beginning to understand a little. Her natural inclination seemed to be putting two people together, and being a divorce lawyer—splitting apart couples—went against her grain. Because of it she divided herself into two distinct parts, thus the compartmentalization. She was an idealist who coped with reality in a very effective way and without compromising what was important to her.

And he was more intrigued than ever.

He slid along the couch until his drawn-up knee touched hers.

"Don't come any closer," she said, a beat too late.

"Why? What are you afraid of?"

She hugged the afghan tighter. "It's just that every time you get close, you . . . we . . ."

With a crooked grin on his face he reached out and caressed her cheek. "Yeah, I know. It's something, isn't it? The way you and I react to each other. Spectacular, actually."

"It doesn't matter. You've already said you're going to call Maggie."

"Do you really want me to call her?" When she didn't answer, he touched the velvet of the robe and then the velvet of her skin at the base of her neck. "I have no intention of calling your friend."

"But why? You said—"

"Samantha," he said softly, gently, "why would I call her? *Why*, when you are completely filling up my mind? *Why*, when I come straight to you whenever I have a few moments of free time?"

His gentleness was throwing her every bit as much as his words. "But you said—"

"I *never* intended to call her. I was only

trying to rattle you, and maybe make you face
a few things."

"Like what?"

"Like *why* you were so intent on matching
me up with someone other than yourself."

She shook her head firmly. "You and I
were never in the cards. It was never even a
possibility."

"Not in your mind, at any rate. But all the
while you were trying to match me up with
one of your friends, you were kissing *me*."

"Only when—"

"Right. Only when I was kissing you,
which—did you happen to notice?—I've been
doing a lot lately. And in case you are unclear
as to what your part in it all was. You were
responding in a way that would drive a weak
man crazy. It only made *me* a little crazy, crazy
enough to keep coming back for more."

What could she say? He was absolutely
right. She responded to his kisses and more.
She couldn't explain it. She'd even been trying
not to think about her response to him. But
the truth was she thought about him all the
time.

"Some people might call you confused,
Samantha."

Or crazy, she thought. "Okay, that's true,
but then others might also call me well-
intentioned. I was only trying to help."

"They might also call you misguided.

With one enormous blind spot where I'm concerned."

"I don't think I've been blind where you're concerned. I was simply trying to do you a favor."

"So then do me a favor." His voice was low and slightly rough. "Kiss me. *You* kiss *me.*"

His mouth was mere inches from hers. She could see the fine pores of his skin, count the individual eyelashes that surrounded his eyes, feel the heat of his breath. She pulled back slightly.

"What's the matter?" he taunted. "Afraid?"

It was the second time he'd accused her of being afraid. "Don't be ridiculous. I simply don't want to kiss you, that's all. Accept it."

He slid his hand around the back of her neck and let his thumb lightly caress her tensed jaw. "I can accept it if it's the truth. I'm just not sure it is, that's all."

"You're not sure because your huge ego won't let you accept it."

He smiled. "Is that it? I don't know. I guess I figure if a woman is constantly on my mind, eating away at my concentration, making me think of very little else—like you are—it has to be reciprocal. Am I wrong? Tell me if I am. Tell me you don't think about me almost constantly since we met, and I promise I'll believe you."

"I . . . I've thought of you." The admission was close to painful. It involved a complete change of mind-set, a change from one that was ordered and easy to deal with.

"That was hard, wasn't it?" His thumb continued to caress. "No one has ever questioned you before. No man has ever challenged you. It makes me think less of my gender, but it also makes me very happy."

"Do you know what you're doing?" she asked carefully.

"I haven't got the faintest idea. I only know that I want very much for you to kiss me." Very gently he pressed his fingers against the back of her neck and applied the lightest of pressure. "Please."

Heat filled her chest, interfering with her breathing. She remembered the way his lips felt on hers and the way she melted inside when he took her in his arms. The memories were strong, and the need to experience all those feelings again was even stronger. She gave in.

She leaned toward him and allowed her lips to touch his, softly at first, wanting to experience the kiss in stages. But the first stage brought heat and hunger, and very quickly she wanted more. Greedily she deepened the kiss, pressing closer and thrusting her tongue into his mouth to rub against his. Why in the world had she thought she could live without this kiss? she wondered. And once she had given in, why had she thought she could handle it?

She couldn't, but it didn't matter. The kiss was everything she wanted. *He* was everything. She felt him push the barrier of the afghan from between them and instead of protesting she slipped her arms around his neck and threaded her fingers up into his hair.

"I like the way you kiss me," he said in a gruff mutter. "It's the same way I kiss you— like I can't get enough."

"Yes." The word came out as a sigh.

His hands ran over her and settled on her breasts, molding her shape through the sensual material. The underside of the velvet slid over her skin, arousing and stimulating her nipples into tight, throbbing buds.

"If I had my way, you'd never stop kissing me, except for those times when I'm kissing you." He bent his head and took a nipple into his mouth, velvet and all.

A cry tore from her throat as pleasure whirled around her and in her and fiery need sank deep into her muscles and bones and then held her in a tense grip.

Frustration and impatience tore at him. He wanted to rip the robe from her body. He wanted to feel her skin beneath his palms, the heat of it, the texture of it, the sheer excitement of it. Of *her*.

"I want you, Samantha. I want to make love to you."

And I want you. She didn't say the words, but with every nerve she possessed she felt the words, and in her own way she expressed them. Clutching at him, she slid lower on the sofa. He followed her, adjusting his weight so that she wasn't taking all of it. Then he slid his hand beneath the robe's hem to her thighs and the silk panties that were the final barrier.

Suddenly he stilled. The pager clipped to his belt was going off.

He pressed the button to quiet it and then lay there for a moment while emotions warred in him. His body was practically screaming for him to ignore the pager, but if he didn't stop to check the number now, it would be hours before he would remember to look at it again. With a soft curse he raised himself and twisted so that he could see the number displayed on the small screen.

"Matthew?"

"I've got to return this call."

She closed her eyes, hard pressed to know whether she wanted to cry in frustration or to give thanks. She'd been moments away from surrendering completely to him. In fact her body still pulsed with the need. But she would be all right. She had to be. Instinctively she knew that their lovemaking would have been wonderful, maybe too wonderful. And that would have been a problem. No, it was better this way. Matthew wasn't the man for her. She would know it if he was.

"Samantha?"

"Go return the call. There's a phone in the kitchen."

"This won't take long." He pressed a hard kiss on her mouth. "Don't move."

Somehow he managed to walk the distance, but every step he took was a painful one. He questioned his sanity in breaking off what was happening between him and Samantha to answer his pager. He questioned the life expectancy of Gage if he ever called him again at such a critical time. He even questioned his dedication to his job. Damn, it had always come first, but giving priority to a story had never before made him feel as if he were coming apart inside.

Almost savagely he punched in the phone number. "Yeah, what is it?" he said when Gage answered.

"I've got more on the woman that had an affair with Barnett, the one that was described as having autumn-colored hair."

"What? Is she a law clerk or a secretary or something like that?"

"No, she's a lawyer."

SIX

Samantha sat up and tugged her robe down over her thighs to her ankles so that she was once again covered. Matthew had told her not to move, but not moving was impossible. She couldn't simply lay there quivering with heat and need, waiting for him to return. She had to pull herself together.

She was appalled. She had come closer than she ever had before to losing complete control over her emotions. And she wasn't merely thinking of the fact that she had nearly made love with Matthew. No. She wasn't a virgin. She had had sex before. Granted her experience wasn't vast, but she was still able to understand that there was something remarkably different about what had just happened between her and Matthew.

Strangely enough, until this moment she

hadn't realized she had been keeping such a tight rein on her emotions.

She was shattered. Because it was the first time she had lost control with a man. And because the loss of control had been with Matthew.

She knew what she had just experienced was important because it should serve as a warning to her, but she didn't completely understand what the warning was about.

She glanced toward the kitchen. He would be back soon and she was going to have to face him. No doubt he would return wanting to take up where they had left off, but she couldn't allow that. She needed to remain cool and firm. There could be no more kisses, no more touches. He would have to leave. And then maybe she could figure out what in the hell was wrong with her.

He appeared in the doorway and she stiffened her spine, ready to resist. "Matthew—"

"Do you have something I can drink?"

"What?" she asked blankly.

He looked around the room distractedly. "Scotch. Something like that."

"No. I only have wine."

"The last thing I need right now is a glass of your strawberry wine. That stuff is way too potent. How about coffee?" Without waiting for her answer he walked to the fireplace, propped his elbow on the mantel, and gazed down at the fire. He needed the support of the mantel. He needed to look at something else besides her.

She stared at him. The man could turn on a dime. One minute he was hot as hell for her and the next he wanted a cup of coffee. "Sure, no problem. As a matter of fact I think I could use a cup of coffee myself, a *strong* one."

Hearing her leave the room, Matthew deliberately kept his back to her. *Dammit.* He still wanted her badly, but Gage's news had been like a cold shower.

A lawyer with autumn-colored hair . . .

Still, he reminded himself, the new information didn't necessarily mean the woman was Samantha. First of all there were numerous female lawyers in and out of the courthouse every week, and surely more than one of them had legs to write home about and hair the color of autumn leaves. It had to be some other woman. *Any* woman besides Samantha.

Gage had planted a seed of doubt, he admitted to himself, but it was only a seed. He had to keep his thinking clear on this. A dead-on accurate description that matched Samantha didn't mean she was the woman who'd had an affair with the judge.

Jealousy. It ate him up to think that Samantha might have slept with Barnett. Or anyone else for that matter. But dammit, Barnett was married!

Samantha reacted to *him* like pure fire. Was it possible that she could react to another man the same way? He already knew she was an expert at compartmentalizing. Could she put Barnett in one compartment and him in another?

Stop, he ordered himself. He had no hard evidence, no proof. He wouldn't let himself condemn her on the basis of a vague description.

On the other hand was he rationalizing that she couldn't be the woman because he wanted her? Yeah, probably. If he had suspected any other woman besides Samantha, he would have been on her trail in an instant. But it *was* Samantha, and he wouldn't let himself make her a serious suspect.

He needed to get away from her, cool down. He couldn't think clearly right now, not when she was with him.

"Here we are."

He heard her behind him and turned to see her bending to place a tray on the ottoman. The scent of coffee drifted to him, but he barely noticed. Her lips looked swollen. There was a slight pinkish tone to her skin where his day's growth of beard had rubbed against her face. She looked like someone who had been thoroughly kissed and nearly made love to. His gut tightened and his blood caught fire again. He wanted her bad and he wanted her now.

"Do you take cream or sugar in your coffee? I forgot." She was so unnerved that if someone asked her name right now, she wasn't sure she would be able to tell him.

He frowned. "I'll fix it myself in a minute. Right now I need to ask you a question I've already asked you."

She took her own coffee cup and sat down, trying to keep her hand from shaking too much. "Something you've already asked me?" Something else she probably wouldn't remember. Her thought processes were completely scrambled. She couldn't ever remember being as confused as she was at this moment. Matthew was brash and abrasive, too much so for comfort, and at the moment she'd like nothing more than for him to make love to her. It didn't make sense. If the week ahead wasn't booked to the walls, she'd take a vacation, somewhere with warm turquoise waters and endless white-sand beaches. Somewhere Matthew wasn't.

"Do you know Judge Richard Barnett?"

The cup she held clattered against its saucer. A small amount of coffee splashed onto her hand. She set the cup and saucer down on the table next to her and sucked the coffee from the back of her hand.

"You've asked me that already."

"I told you I had. Do you know him?"

"Why in heaven's name are you bringing him up? Was that phone call about him?"

He let out a long breath. "Just answer my question, Samantha. Do you or don't you know him?"

She eyed him warily. "Why should I answer a question I've already answered?"

"Because it's a simple question. And because you never really gave me a definitive answer."

"I think I did. I said that everyone knows of him, but that he and I work in different courts."

"So your answer is that you know *of* him, but that you don't really know him personally?"

She shrugged. "Well, I mean, what's personal? I might say hello to him if I passed him in the hall—"

He exploded. "For God's sake, Samantha! Will you for once just give me a straight answer?"

She stood and eyed him levelly. "I just did. Now, please leave."

"Well, well, well—here you are again asking me to leave. This is getting real monotonous, Samantha."

"Except this time I didn't invite you here in the first place." Without waiting for his reply, she headed for the front door.

He stared at her. She wasn't being honest with him and he knew it. Worse, something in him kept him from wanting to press her further. It was so unlike him. Hell, maybe it was better if he didn't know the truth. He didn't want to think of her writhing naked on a bed with Barnett over her. The mere thought made him want to do something violent.

The problem was he'd also like to make love to her until she couldn't lie to him, couldn't think of another man. *And*, he forcibly reminded himself, he still had no proof that she was the woman. Maybe she had another reason for not telling him the truth. Maybe . . . yeah, right, he thought morosely. If he could only come up with that reason.

Suddenly he realized he was alone in the room. He found her standing by the front door, holding it open.

"You really *are* anxious to get rid of me, aren't you?"

"It's been a long day and I'm tired."

"And you want to go to bed?"

"Yes."

"Funny. I could have sworn that's where we were heading just a short time ago."

"You're the one who got the phone call."

"Are you saying you would have been willing?" It was a stupid thing to ask. They both had been willing. But he wanted to nettle her, to make her feel as bad as he did right now. He was being childish. And he was letting her get to him as no woman ever had.

"I'm saying I want to go to bed now. Alone."

He was tempted to stay and bait her some more, but in truth he was tired too. He felt emotionally drained. And he *had* gotten the phone call. He needed to be by himself and see if he could regain at least a portion of his objectivity. But he couldn't leave her quite yet. "The wedding is tomorrow," he said. "Are you going to be there?"

Wearily she combed her fingers through her hair. "I've told Leona I'll come, and I won't let her down. The day is too important to her."

"Maybe we could go together." What in the hell was he doing? *Distance*, he reminded himself. He needed *distance* from her. Going to the wedding with her would likely be the worst possible thing he could do. "Would you like to go with me?"

She shook her head. "No, I don't think so."

Disappointment lanced through him. A muscle clenched in his jaw. "Then I'll see you there."

"Good-bye, Matthew."

"Good-bye, Samantha."

He started out the door, but as he passed

her, he stopped and compulsively reached out for her.

Samantha flattened her hands against his chest, but she couldn't bring herself to push him away. And then he brought his mouth down on hers in a shattering, thorough kiss that was filled with assurance and knowledge. It was a kiss meant to indelibly stamp possession, and she felt its effects all the way to the ends of her fingertips. As always she was completely overwhelmed. She had no idea how long the kiss lasted. Sensation replaced time. She clung to him, relinquishing her will and responding. And when he finally raised his head, his hard gaze seared her every bit as much as his kiss had done.

"*Now* I'll leave," he said thickly.

She shut the door after him, then leaned back weakly against it.

What was she going to do?

Saturday morning dawned clear, bright, and golden. Gazing out of the window, Samantha managed a small smile for the day. Leona and Alfred would have a beautiful day for their wedding. She was glad, though she knew they wouldn't care what the weather was. In fact they were so excited about joining their lives together for the rest of their lives, she wasn't sure they would even notice what the weather was today. She had known almost immediately that they were meant for each other.

How could she have been so right about them and so off on Matthew?

He had accused her of having an enormous blind spot where he was concerned, and she had to admit there was something to what he said. Putting Alfred and Leona together had been the right thing for her to do. Unfortunately the act had brought Matthew into her life.

Unfortunately? She paused and backtracked with her thinking. Did she really believe it was a bad thing that she had met Matthew? He had brought a special kind of excitement into her life, along with turmoil, and that left her unsure whether his effect on her was good or bad. Did it really even matter what it was? Quite simply he was in her life, and there didn't seem to be anything she could do to change that fact, even if she wanted to.

Unfortunately—*there was that thought again*—Matthew's presence brought complications because of Richard Barnett.

By nature she was a straightforward person. To be anything else was extremely hard on her, but it was inbred in her that loyalties were to be honored. And Richard had been in her life for years, Matthew only days. She turned away from the window and walked to the phone. She had two important calls to make.

What in the hell was Richard Barnett doing in a park?

From his vantage point in his car Matthew frowned at the sight of the distinguished judge sitting at a picnic table all by himself. He was obviously waiting for someone.

Luck had played a large part in his being here, Matthew remembered. He had driven to the courthouse and was preparing to park, when he saw the judge driving away. Seizing the opportunity, he had followed him, and now he was parked a discreet distance away, waiting, just like the judge.

It was ten o'clock in the morning, and the wedding started at one. He hoped whoever the judge was meeting wouldn't be late.

Just as he was thinking that, a car drew to a stop at the curb closest to the judge.

Great. And the only passenger was a woman. She looked familiar. Who . . . ?

No. It couldn't be!

He punched open the glove compartment, grabbed the small binoculars he always carried with him, and focused them on the woman as she walked toward the judge.

Samantha.

His stomach turned over and his arms lost their strength. He lowered the binoculars until his hands were resting in his lap.

God, he didn't want to see this. He shut his eyes and took a deep breath. His heart was beating a mile a minute, and for a moment he actually felt as if he were going to throw up.

Dammit, Samantha, why didn't you tell me the truth?

He took several deep breaths, waiting for his world to right itself, then again raised the binoculars to his eyes. She was sitting very close to Barnett, holding his hand. Their expressions were intense, serious.

His grip tightened on the glasses. Samantha appeared upset. She looked as if she cared too much for the man sitting next to her. The body language of the two shouted intimacy, as if she was used to holding his hand and he was used to being close to her.

He dropped the glasses onto the seat beside him and rubbed his eyes. For once in his life he was glad he couldn't read lips. It went against every journalistic instinct he had, but he didn't want to know what the two of them were talking about.

Irrationally he felt betrayed.

And, he acknowledged, his feelings *were* definitely irrational.

He and Samantha had known each other only a short time. No words of love had been exchanged. No vows or promises. Only kisses. Deep, hot, long kisses that made him want to make love to her forever.

Once again he wiped his hands over his eyes, but he couldn't wipe out the sight of Samantha and the judge. Without the binoculars the two of them appeared small, even blurred. But the distance didn't prevent him from seeing when they stood and embraced.

With a loud, angry curse he slammed the heel of his hand against the steering wheel.

The manicured backyard of Alfred's estate was the site for Alfred and Leona's wedding. Gazing over the group of people in attendance, he estimated there were a little over a hundred guests. Leona had told him that only the people most important to her and Alfred would be invited. He knew his aunt thought the world of Samantha, but she wasn't there.

Gold, brown, and russet-colored leaves decorated the trees around them. Alfred stood beneath an arched trellis covered in various kinds of lilies and chrysanthemums, talking to the minister. Ribbons that echoed the colors of the leaves had been threaded through the flowers and formed into bows that ended in flowing streamers. It was an autumn-colored wedding, and the colors reminded him of Samantha.

Where was she?

He absently rubbed the injured heel of his hand. Off to one side a string quartet played, but the lovely music did nothing to soothe his nerves or his temper.

His shock at seeing Samantha with Barnett had worn off, leaving cold, hard anger. Logically he understood that the anger wasn't rational, but there didn't seem to be anything he could do about it. His gut and his heart were involved. Analyzing himself wasn't his style, but soon, for his own peace of mind, he needed to try to understand how Samantha had gotten so important to him so quickly.

He glanced at Alfred. He was chatting and smiling, not looking at all nervous. Leona wasn't either, he knew. He had checked in with her before he had taken his seat, and she had looked radiantly happy and completely relaxed. She deserved to be. He didn't regret his initial fears and suspicions regarding Alfred, but he couldn't be more pleased that they had proved groundless. He wished he was as happy about what was going on in his own life.

He glanced at his watch. The ceremony was due to start any minute. Dammit, where was Samantha?

Then he saw her. She was wearing a gold silk suit. The jacket had small, fabric-covered buttons that started at the bottom of the deep V of the neckline and descended down its front. Teaming together to accentuate her long legs were gold high-heeled pumps, a skirt inches above her knees, and hose that shimmered. Her autumn-colored hair was pulled back and tied with a wide gold ribbon. Small, clear crystals glinted at her ears and threw sunlight onto her face.

And she was walking down the aisle formed by the two groups of chairs, her hand on a stranger's arm.

She had brought a date.

He surged to his feet, prepared to do something, but without a clear idea as to what or why. The first chords of a beautiful melody sounded, and everyone around stood, including Samantha and her date now on the other side of the aisle from him. Leona, he realized, was starting down the aisle.

He was shaking. What was wrong with him? He folded his hands together and willed himself to stop. Samantha had lied to him, but she certainly wasn't the first person ever to do so. She had brought a date to a place she had known for sure he would be—so what?

Ah, hell, he'd even asked her to come with him and all the time she had planned to come with someone else. But she was entitled to come with whomever she wished.

No, she wasn't, he immediately corrected himself. She might *think* she was entitled, but there was no way she'd ever be able to convince him of that. Not after everything that had happened between them. She had to have known it would infuriate him to see her with another man here. So what was she doing? And why?

Leona drew even with him and sent him a special smile. Summoning his self-possession, he returned her smile, knowing that if he didn't, she would wonder why. Her day was not going to be ruined, he vowed. Not by him and not by Samantha.

The ceremony proceeded, and he used the time to pull himself together. And as he did so, a dark anger took possession of him. By the time the wedding was over, he felt icily calm. He knew exactly what he was going to do.

The first thing he did was to go to his aunt. "I'm so happy for you, Aunt Leona." He bent down and kissed her cheek.

She smiled up at him. "And you weren't upset that I didn't ask you to give me away this time?"

"Not at all. Why would you think that?"

She patted his cheek. "I don't know. You look a little pale. Are you upset about something?"

His aunt was sharp. "Nothing could be farther from the truth. And as for giving you away, I've done it twice. I think that's more than enough."

Leona beamed. "I'm so absolutely certain that this marriage is right that this time I decided I didn't need anyone to give me away. I wanted to go to Alfred by myself."

"I think that's wonderful." He squeezed her hand. "Do I get a dance?"

"You certainly do. The second one, right after Alfred."

Alfred moved away from a nearby group of well-wishers and joined them. "Did I hear my bride speak my name?"

Leona laughed. "I was just telling Matthew I wanted him to have the second dance."

"Does that mean I get only one dance?"

Leona gazed adoringly up at her new bridegroom. "You and I are going to spend the rest of our lives dancing."

His gaze was soft with love as it rested on her. "Why don't we start right now?" He signaled to the string quartet, and they struck up "It Had to Be You."

With a genuine smile Matthew watched them move onto the dance floor that had been placed over a portion of the lawn. No matter what else happened, he would be forever grateful to Samantha for introducing his aunt to Alfred. But the time was drawing closer when he would deal with Samantha.

"Hello, Matthew."

At the sound of her voice he turned, his smile vanishing. "Hello, Samantha."

She still had her hand on the arm of her date, a *very good-looking* date.

"Matthew, this is my friend, Sloan Michaels."

The man held out his hand, and Matthew hesitated only briefly. Leona happened to be looking his way. "Nice to meet you, Sloan," he said, taking the other man's hand.

"Likewise. I'm a great admirer of your work."

"Thanks."

"It was a beautiful wedding, wasn't it?" Samantha said into the awkward silence that followed.

She was nervous. The knowledge made him feel better. "Very. What about you, Sloan?" he asked, his tone barbed. "Did you enjoy it?"

Sloan nodded pleasantly. "I did, even though I've never had the pleasure of meeting the bride and groom. They look very happy."

"So you don't know Alfred or Leona? You're just here as Samantha's date?"

"That's right."

"Have you two known each other long?"

Samantha's laugh was jittery. "You'll have to forgive Matthew, Sloan. He sometimes doesn't know where to draw the line between his journalistic career and his off-duty life."

Matthew bared his teeth in an obviously fake smile. "Oh, I always know exactly where the line is. The problem is that where you're concerned, the line keeps moving."

"Is it my fault you can't keep up with where it is?"

His eyes narrowed. "Yes, now that you mention it, I think it is."

With a puzzled expression on his handsome face Sloan looked from one to the other. "Is this a serious disagreement between you two?"

"Those are the only kind of disagreements we ever have—right, Samantha?"

"I wouldn't say that we disagree."

"Really? Then what would you call what you and I do?" It was a question loaded with sarcasm and double meaning, and he could tell by her expression that she recognized it.

But she merely shrugged. "We have discussions where we happen to have two differing points of view."

"*Heated* discussions," he said. "*Heated.* In fact just about everything we do could be characterized as heated. Wouldn't you agree, Samantha?" He smiled with satisfaction as she colored. Out on the dance floor Leona motioned to him. "Excuse me," he said before Samantha could gather herself together to reply.

He tried to relax while he danced with his aunt and to concentrate on what she was saying so he could make appropriate responses.

He must have succeeded because Leona chattered away happily. "Aunt Leona, I can honestly say I've never seen you more beautiful."

"Thank you, darling. I can't tell you what it means to me to have you here today. For a while there I wasn't sure you'd come or, quite frankly, that I'd have you here."

He threw back his head and laughed. "Unless you planned to hire an entire security force, you wouldn't have been able to keep me away. I love you, Aunt Leona. I'll always be here for you."

"And I love you, but now that I have Alfred, I want you to have someone special too. Melissa was a long time ago."

He mentally groaned. They had had this discussion many times before. "Aunt Leona—"

"Now, just shush because I know what I'm talking about." She glanced over his shoulder. "You know, I had high hopes for you and Samantha, but there she is with someone else. How could you have let that happen?"

"Believe it or not, some things are beyond even my control."

"Yes, but letting Samantha get away was a big mistake, in my opinion."

"I didn't let her get away, Aunt Leona. I never had her in the first place."

"An even bigger mistake."

He smiled ruefully. "It's nothing for you

to worry about, and certainly not today. Now, why don't you tell me where that groom of yours is going to take you on your honeymoon."

She looked shocked. "Certainly not! There are tried-and-true reasons why a honeymoon destination should be kept a secret, and I happen to believe in every one of them."

He laughed again, truly amused. "Are you honestly afraid I'll follow and pester you? Or maybe sneak into your bedroom and short-sheet your bed?"

"I will *not* discuss my bed with you, young man, and if you even think about short-sheeting my bed or pulling any other prank, I'll—"

He chuckled. "It's all right, Aunt Leona. I was just kidding.".

"Well, stop it right now. Do you still have that number I gave you in case of an emergency?"

"Yes."

"Fine. Then I don't want to hear from you unless it *is* an emergency."

"Yes, Aunt Leona. Whatever you say, Aunt Leona."

The reception continued. The champagne flowed. The quartet serenaded and entertained. And Matthew bided his time.

He stood by himself on the terrace, looking down on the dance floor and watched the ebb and flow of the reception. For his aunt's sake he was forcing himself to be patient, when in reality it was the last thing he felt like being.

Samantha stayed on the dance floor practically all afternoon, and he watched. . . .

He watched the shape of her legs as she danced and the way the sun struck gold highlights into her hair. He watched the way her body fit against Sloan's. He watched the way Sloan's hand curved possessively at her waist.

He watched and he watched until he couldn't stand watching anymore and then he made his move.

SEVEN

A quiver of alarm and anticipation raced through Samantha as she saw Matthew descend the terrace steps to the dance floor and begin to thread his way through the dancers to her. Atop Sloan's shoulder her hand balled into a fist. She had known it was only a matter of time.

All afternoon she had been aware of him as he leaned casually against the terrace balustrade. Once again he had reminded her of a tiger, lazing in the afternoon sun, but this time conserving his power as he kept an eye on his prey. And there had been no doubt in her mind exactly who his prey was. It was her. Across the distance that separated them, she had felt the strength and intensity of his focus.

Was he angry because she had brought Sloan? She was sure of it. She even understood that anger. She had known when she called Sloan this morning and asked him to come with her that she was tempting fate where Matthew was concerned. She had known and had still felt compelled to bring Sloan with her. Was there something else Matthew was angry about? She had no idea. But then did he really need anything else? Together the two of them were like a volcano that simmered just below the surface, erupting at almost regular intervals. And volcanos were a force of nature outside man's control.

Briefly she contemplated leaving, but Leona wouldn't have understood, and ultimately she decided she didn't want to give Matthew the satisfaction of knowing she had left because of him. And so she braced for what was to come and didn't have to wait long at all.

Reaching her, he clamped his hand around her wrist, wrenched her from Sloan's arms, and swung her into his. She probably should be afraid, but there was only wariness and excitement, two emotions he never failed to evoke in her.

"I'm cutting in now."

It was an order instead of a request, and no one who heard it thought of it as anything else. Certainly not her, caught and held not only by his arms but by the concentrated force of his personality.

"Samantha?"

She glanced at an obviously surprised Sloan and realized that for a moment she had forgotten his presence. "It's all right," she said in an attempt to smooth things over with him. "I'll see you in a few minutes."

Uncertainly Sloan glanced between the two of them. "Okay, then, I'll get us a drink and be waiting for you on the terrace."

"Don't worry about Samantha," Matthew said to Sloan, without once taking his gaze from her. "I'll take good care of her." His voice carried a rough intimacy that had Sloan casting one final glance at them.

Samantha waited until he had left, then verbally pounced on Matthew. "What in the hell do you think you're doing?"

"Dancing with you. What do *you* think I'm doing?"

"Being incredibly rude. There's no telling what Sloan is thinking."

"Poor Sloan. He'll simply have to be brave and get over it."

His casual cruelty nearly took her breath away. Her breasts were flattened against his chest, and the hard muscles of his thighs and pelvis were pressed against her lower body. Equal parts of anger and sexuality were coming off him in waves, creating a force field that surrounded her and prevented her from moving away from him. Heat was twisting through her, coming in contact with nerves buried

deep inside her, igniting them and bringing
them to fiery life. Still she couldn't allow him
to know the effect he was having on her.
"Sloan doesn't deserve to be treated shab-
bily."

"Then, Samantha, you should have left
him at home today. Bringing him here was
setting him up for shabby treatment and
more, and you know it."

"I didn't set him up for anything. My invitation from Leona read, 'Samantha McMillan
and guest.' Sloan is my guest."

"And what else is he?" His eyes glinted
with hard, dark lights. "And did you really
think he would keep me away from you?"

She had hoped for exactly that, she acknowledged to herself, and called herself a
coward for doing so. She'd even known she
was being a coward when she had picked up
the phone this morning and called Sloan. And
even then some part of her had known the
tactic wouldn't work.

The music was slow and romantic, and
Matthew moved with surprising grace. She
felt his strength as he held her locked against
his muscled body and his arousal that pressed
into her. She was shocked and excited. He
made her feel extremes, from raw hunger to
quivering need. And she was on a dance floor,
of all places. With an inner groan she acknowledged that at this moment he was more

dangerous to her than at any time since she had known him. And she had to fight to keep herself from sagging against him.

"Is he your lover?"

The shock of the question was almost equal to the shock of feeling his hard body against hers. She was a woman with a law practice of her own who routinely helped people, but at this moment she felt badly in need of help herself. "That's none of your business!"

"Who the hell cares whether it's my business or not? I don't. Tell me—did you let him into your bed? A place, I might add, you've managed quite easily to keep me away from."

"You're the one who got the phone call and then asked for coffee."

His eyes narrowed on her. "Is that a complaint?"

"No, it's the truth."

"That's good, Samantha. I like the truth. I spend a lot of my time trying to find it. At last maybe we'll be able to find some common ground."

"Is there some point to all of this?" She looked away from him, but found nothing on which she could focus.

"Yes, there's a point. You look beautiful, by the way. Sexy."

She wished he hadn't said that. It reminded her that it was *him* she had thought of when she had chosen what she would wear today. She had wondered if he would like it, and she had wondered if he would think she was sexy in it.

"In fact just looking at you takes my breath away."

Her hand rested on the shoulder of his navy-blue suit. She would have to slide her fingers only an inch along his shoulder to touch his neck; a little farther and she would be able to feel the thick vitality of his hair. Someone near them laughed, a carefree sound that contrasted with the inner tension that coiled and twisted its way through her. In truth *he* was taking *her* breath away.

"Are you going to answer my question?"

She looked at him, her brow furrowed. "I'm having a problem keeping track of this conversation."

"Only because you don't like the subject. Stay with me on this and we'll be through it in no time at all."

"Somehow I don't believe that."

"I'm crushed."

"I don't believe that either."

"Distrust is a terrible thing, Samantha. It can be every bit as destructive as the most powerful corrosive. I know because I have it too, and I don't like it. It's why I'm trying to get some things straightened out between us."

She looked at him in disbelief. "And *Sloan* is one of those things?"

"I chose to start with him. He bothers me, but then you knew he would. Admit it, Samantha—you brought him with you today in the hope he would protect you from me."

"I enjoy spending time with Sloan. He's relaxing. He doesn't interrogate me the way you do."

"I do other things to you." His voice dropped to a croon. "If you don't remember, I'll be happy to show you."

The mere idea sent heated shivers through her. She drew a quiet, but ragged breath. "That won't be necessary."

He considered her flushed cheeks, then said softly, "He's only one man, Samantha. If you were really serious about protecting yourself from me, you should have brought an armed division."

Something she should have obviously considered, she thought, trying to find humor in the situation but failing. "You think a lot of yourself, Matthew. You're really not that dangerous." She was well aware that her statement directly contradicted her previous thoughts on him. Bravado. She was trying for bravado and failing miserably.

"I agree. I'd rather let a fly out the door than kill it. But on some level you must think

I'm dangerous. Otherwise you wouldn't have brought Sloan."

"All of this because I wanted to come here with someone else and I turned you down?"

"All of this because you didn't like the idea of being here alone with me."

"Don't look now, Matthew, but there are a lot of other guests at this wedding."

"You know what I'm talking about, and I frankly don't get it. Help me out here. Why did you think you needed protection from me in the first place?"

"I . . ." She wasn't certain what she should say. What could she say that would be safe? And the truth? In reference to Matthew, safety and truth didn't seem compatible.

"Haven't I always stopped when you said stop? Haven't I treated you with kid gloves?"

Her eyes widened in amazement. "You must be kidding. I feel as if I have bruises all over my body." Even as she said it, she knew it was foolish. Still it was exactly the way she felt.

"How strange when I've barely touched you."

Her brow pleated. "You've been assaulting me, metaphorically, since that first day we met."

"Sweetheart," he said, his voice a rough rasp that brought fire to her skin, "you don't even begin to understand what it would be like to be assaulted by me, metaphorically or any other way."

"You're out of your mind," she said, her tone barely above a whisper.

"I think you're right."

The quartet was playing the old Rodgers and Hart song "Bewitched." How appropriate, he thought grimly, his gaze drifting down her throat to the V of her suit jacket, where part of her cleavage showed. She had totally bewitched and enchanted him. He was out of his mind. What other answer could there be?

His gaze seared, his touch invaded, his questions threatened. She tried to pull away from him, but his arms held her fast. "I don't want to dance with you any longer. I need to get back to Sloan."

"You *must* be kidding."

Her head snapped back. "What do you want from me, Matthew?"

"There are quite a few answers I could give to that, but let's start with the truth, something I've been trying to get from you from the beginning. Are you even capable of telling the truth, Samantha?"

His words felt like serrated blades against her too sensitive skin. "Oh, nice, Matthew. Nice. You're attacking my character in the middle of your aunt's lovely wedding party. I suppose you think you have a reason for doing this."

"A very good reason."

"Would you like to share that reason, or are you having too much fun accusing me of being a liar?"

"Fun? You're mistaken, Samantha. I'm not having any fun at all."

"You could have fooled me. Now, excuse me, I want to get back to Sloan."

"You've already said that. You don't need to repeat it. I'm quick. I can usually get things the first time."

"Then either tell me what it is you want from me or let me go."

"Since I'm not about to do the latter, I guess I'd better do the former. Okay, here it is —I was wondering what you did this morning."

She missed a step. His arms caught her against him, bringing her so close, it seemed she could feel every muscle and sinew in his body. "This morning?"

"You see? Already you're avoiding the question."

"No, it's just that . . ." It was a strange question for him to ask, and her mind raced to figure out the reason.

"Just what?"

Damn. She was angry—at him, yes, but she was even more angry at herself for letting him get to her.

"Silence, Samantha? What am I going to

do with you? You've become a big problem to me. You lie to me and then you get in my head and refuse to leave."

"I have no idea what you're talking about."

"Ah, see there—you're lying again. What do you think I should do about that?"

"You only think it's a lie because you don't want to believe me."

"What in the hell do you want me to believe? You haven't told me anything. And the question I asked was such a simple one. What did you do this morning?"

Maybe the question had been simple, but the answer wasn't, and neither was he. He was too close, too strong, too compellingly attractive. He thought she was a problem to him, but it was nothing compared to what he was becoming to her. "You're right. It is a simple question, so simple in fact, I don't know why you're asking it, but okay—this morning I got ready to come here."

His brows shot up. "I've got to hand it to you. You're good, *very* good."

"That's what I did—I got ready to come here."

"Of course you did. Now tell me what *else* you did."

"No, Matthew. I don't have to tell you one more thing. I answered the one question, I'm not answering another."

His brows arched. *"Wow.* I must have hit a nerve. Why?"

"Just leave me the hell alone."

"That would be impossible." He drew an uneven breath as he gazed down at her. "Sad but there it is. And you know what else is sad? I want to believe in you so damned bad, I'm hurting like hell with the need."

The pain in his voice caught and held her, softening her resistance, her body, and her heart. "Matthew . . ."

"What?" His voice was almost a croon. "Tell me something that will make me feel better, but please, Samantha, please make it the truth."

She felt utterly helpless, dazed, trapped between his hard gaze and his soft voice. "I'm sorry . . . I'm sorry . . . I've lost track . . . I don't know what we're talking about."

"Don't you? Then I'm the one who should apologize. I must be doing something very wrong."

She registered the disappointment in his tone and found it as moving as his pain. What was she going to do?

He glanced over her shoulder. "Sloan is up on the terrace looking extremely worried. You'd better give him one of those remarkable smiles of yours, because it's all he's going to get from you today."

Thinking of Sloan was impossible for her

now. Her entire focus was on the man who held her. He was important to her, she realized. *Very* important. Too important. She didn't want to disappoint him and she didn't want to hurt him, but she couldn't tell him the truth. "Matthew, please can't you simply trust me?"

"Trust you? Why? Can you promise me you'll always tell me the truth? Can you promise me you'll never carve out my heart and hand it to me on a platter?"

Again she wasn't precisely sure what he was talking about. "I can promise you the latter simply because you would never let me near your heart."

He muttered a violent oath. "What the hell! Let's get out of here. I need to be alone with you. I need to hear you tell me the truth, even if it's only to hear you say the sky is blue and the grass is green."

"Matthew, I'm so sorry. I wish things were different, but—"

"Would all the single ladies please come forward?" Alfred called out. "My lovely wife is going to throw the bouquet."

"Oh, Lord," she said. "We can't leave. Sloan is here, and there's Leona—"

"Samantha!" Leona waved to her. "*Samantha!* Come closer!"

"I've got to go up there." She pulled free of his arms, but couldn't dislodge his grip on her hand. She looked back at him. "I've got to *go*, Matthew."

"I told you," he said, biting out each word from between clenched teeth. "I'm quick. You don't have to repeat things." He turned and drew her with him through the crowd until they were at the base of the terrace with Leona and Alfred above them.

"All you single ladies get ready," Alfred said gaily.

With a significant look at Samantha, Leona turned her back and tossed the bouquet.

Aware that Leona had thrown the bouquet to her, Samantha watched it arc high in the air above them.

Matthew leaned down, put his mouth to her ear, and whispered, "Richard Barnett had an affair with a woman lawyer who does business in the courthouse, and she's been described as having legs to write home about and autumn-colored hair. Sound familiar to you?"

Stunned, Samantha swung her head around to look at him. Leona yelled something at her. The bouquet of white lilacs and gold chrysanthemums hit her in the chest and landed on the ground at her feet. And still she couldn't look away from Matthew.

He was smiling at her, but the smile didn't reach his eyes. "I thought it might," he murmured. After a moment he bent down, picked up the bouquet, and handed it to her. "You would make a beautiful autumn bride, but I hope you don't think Barnett is going to divorce his wife and marry you. Say something to Aunt Leona."

She was speechless. She wasn't even certain she could move. She looked down at the bouquet she was now holding but couldn't feel its weight in her hand. All around her, people were talking and laughing, but she couldn't make out any of the words. She heard Leona's voice. She knew she should say something to her, but she couldn't think of what. She felt someone come up beside her and touch her arm. She turned and saw Sloan. Lord, she'd forgotten all about him!

She wished everyone would go away and leave her alone with Matthew. She wanted to tell him he was wrong about her and Richard. She wanted to. But she couldn't.

"Samantha?" It was Leona, leaning over the balustrade, looking at her worriedly.

"Have a wonderful honeymoon." Her voice sounded thready, but apparently Leona heard her.

She smiled. "Thank you, we will. Good-bye, Matthew. I'll call you when we get back."

Matthew raised his hand, but with his other hand he kept a firm hold on Samantha's. "Good-bye, Aunt Leona, Alfred."

The crowd surged after the newly married couple, packets of birdseed in their hands.

Very quickly the backyard emptied, and then only the three of them were left.

Matthew turned his hard gaze on Sloan. "I hope you don't mind, but Samantha and I have to leave. We have some important things we need to sort out." He felt her hand jerk against his, but whether it was in surprise or protest, he couldn't tell because she didn't speak.

Sloan turned to her. "Samantha?"

She wasn't going to get out of this, she thought dully. Matthew wouldn't let her. All that was left for her to do was to make as graceful an exit as possible. She couldn't tell him everything, but in fairness she would tell him what she could. "I'm sorry, Sloan. Matthew's right. We do have some things to sort out. Thank you for coming with me today. I really appreciate it and it was a lot of fun. I'll talk to you on Monday."

Sloan looked from her to Matthew and then back to her. "If you're sure?"

"I'm positive. Thank you again."

He nodded. "Then I'll see you on Monday."

Matthew was still as he watched Sloan walk away. He was feeling so many emotions, it was hard for him to keep them all under control. Frustration, anger, desire—they roiled together in him, seeming to be one and the same.

Slowly he lifted her hand so that he could see it. It was small-boned with long, slender fingers, and her nails were short and clear, bare of polish, as they had been that first night at her house. He thought of the vegetables she had grown and the strawberry wine she'd made. And he thought of how his skin had felt those few times when she'd touched him. "Let's get out of here."

"Where are we going?"

"I haven't got the faintest idea."

But he did. He drove straight to her house.

In the entrance hall he caught her upper arms and propelled her back against the wall. "Did you have an affair with Richard Barnett?"

"No!" Pushing against him, she tried to break free, but like shoving against a brick wall, there was no give. "What are you doing?"

"I'm trying to find out if you were the woman Barnett had an affair with."

She stopped struggling and looked at him, exasperated and indignant. "By holding me against the wall? And exactly how long have you been laboring under that false idea?"

"Long enough to make me crazy." He dropped his arms away and shoved his fingers through his hair.

"Why didn't you just ask me?"

He turned a burning gaze on her. "Because as a journalist I never reveal everything I know. And I did ask you if you knew him—remember?—but you never gave me a definitive answer."

When it came to Richard, it seemed they both had their own agendas. She just wished Matthew's agenda didn't scare her so much. Even though he no longer held her, she still leaned against the wall, grateful for the support. Why did everything with Matthew have to be such a battle? "I didn't have an affair with Richard."

"Do you swear it?"

"I don't have to swear to anything. This isn't a court of law." She badly wanted him to believe her, but contrarily she resented having to convince him.

"Dammit, I *want* to believe you."

"Then do it! Believe me!"

"You do know him, don't you?"

"I told you—"

With a curse he reached for her again. "I'd rather kiss you than have you lie to me one more time," he said gruffly. He brought his mouth down on hers, grinding his lips into hers, venting both his frustration and his need for her, need that had eaten at him practically from the first moment he had laid eyes on her. It was all useless. He wanted her so badly, he was almost to the point of not caring whether she lied to him or not. He'd been accused of getting caught up in his work and losing himself, but he had never been accused of getting caught up in a woman. With Samantha everything was different, though. He had the terrible feeling he *had* lost himself.

She was dimly aware that the sexual attraction between them was nearly out of control. Heat, need, and pleasure flooded through her, all at the same time. But he thought she was a liar, and she couldn't stand the idea that there were things that needed to be resolved between them. Her fingers dug into the fabric of his jacket, and a sound of protest erupted from her throat.

Dammit, he didn't want to stop. He wanted nothing more than to find the nearest bed and make love to her. But he had heard the sound and eased away from her.

A thick, shining strand of her hair had come loose from the golden bow and hung down the side of her face. Gently he brushed it behind her ear. "What is it?"

"We need to talk."

"You think we can? You want to try again with our little conversation?"

She laughed weakly. "Is that what we were having?"

"We were *attempting* to have one. Attempting is what you and I do a lot of."

She drew a shaky breath and nodded.
"Let's go into the living room."

"What difference does it make where we are?"

"I need to sit down."

But once in the living room, she didn't sit.
He did. And watched as she paced back and
forth in front of the fireplace. "This can't be
that hard, Samantha."

"It is because it involves a loyalty, and I
don't take loyalties lightly."

He struggled with his temper. *He* wanted
her loyalties, dammit. "Then let's just start
with something simple. Tell me what your relationship is with Barnett."

A glance at him informed her that he had
unknotted his tie so that it hung loose and had
unbuttoned several of his shirt's top buttons.
Tension fairly radiated from him, along with a
sexuality barely held in check. She could still
feel the imprint of his lips on hers, taste him
in her mouth. She was utterly hopeless where
he was concerned.

"Richard and I are friends," she finally
said, taking off her clip-on earrings and absently rubbing her lobes. "Actually he was a
friend of my father's, and when my father
died, Richard became my mentor in law
school. His advice and support over the years
have been invaluable to me, and we've grown
to be very good friends."

"Why didn't you tell me this when I first asked?"

The quietly asked question did nothing to dispel the electricity of charged emotions that arced between them. It would be dangerous to light a match in the room, she concluded. The room and everything in it including them would go up in flames.

"I didn't have a clue why you wanted to know, and I thought I should find out what was going on before I unwittingly gave anything away to you."

"So that means you were suspicious of me."

His flat voice was at odds with his coiled alertness. "Yes, but you could also look at it another way too. I respect your investigative journalistic abilities to the extent that I thought my friend might need protecting from you."

"And so you lied to me."

"No. I kept things from you, but I never lied."

"It's called lying by omission, Samantha. I'm sure it happens to you a lot in your work. I know it does in mine."

"Then you shouldn't be shocked that I did it."

"No, I'm not shocked. Just disappointed, because when it comes to you and me, I was hoping . . ." His voice trailed off, but his meaning hung in the air between them.

She felt as if he had punched her. She turned away and stared blindly at a picture of her father and mother on the mantel. Their marriage hadn't been a happy one, but her father had been a man of high principles, and by his words and actions he had conveyed to her that Richard was too. She still believed that. But the knowledge didn't make it any easier to keep things from Matthew. "I'm sorry you feel that way."

"I'll tell you what. I'll give you a chance to redeem yourself."

She swung around, irrationally angry and hurt. "I don't need to redeem myself with you or anyone else."

"No? Okay, then, tell me what were you doing with Barnett this morning?"

She stilled. "This morning?"

"Dammit, Samantha, just admit it. You had a meeting with him in the park this morning, a meeting that looked downright *cozy.*"

"Looked?" His unexpected knowledge had thrown her off balance. "How do you know?" Her eyes widened in disbelief. "Matthew? Were you *following* me?"

"No, but obviously I should have been. It might have saved me some time. But, stupid me, I was following the judge. Then again you both ended up in the same place, didn't you?"

"It's not what you think. I told you Richard and I are just friends."

"Friends who apparently share secrets. I gather he knows I'm on his trail?"

"Yes, I told him."

"What a lucky man to have such a helpful friend."

"Matthew—"

"Exactly how helpful are you? Did you help him out in bed too?"

"He didn't have an affair with me," she said dully, crossing her arms beneath her breasts. "It was with someone else."

He sprang off the couch and with two long strides was standing in front of her. "Someone else whose description is a dead ringer for you. Some people might think that this mentor-friend of yours has quite an interesting fixation on you."

"*Stop it!* It's not like that. Richard is a good and decent and honorable man."

"Who just happened to have cheated on his wife. Tell me, is she your friend too?"

"Yes, yes, she is! And they do have a good marriage. In twenty-seven years of marriage Richard made one mistake, and he bitterly regrets it."

"I just bet he does. After all, his one little indiscretion is probably going to bring him down off the bench for good."

"He knows that."

"But does he accept it or is he trying to cover up?"

"I can't tell you any more, Matthew."

"Tell me any *more*? Sweetheart, you haven't told me a damned thing except that you're not the woman he slept with, which, by the way, after that touching little scene in the park this morning I'm still having trouble believing."

Her eyes flashed angrily. "I'm telling you the truth. Richard and I have never slept together. He's been incredibly supportive of me over the years, and I owe him a lot, but we have never, ever slept together. Our relationship is more like father and daughter."

He stared at her, his expression bleak. "You have no idea how much I want to believe you."

"So what's keeping you from it?"

"Jealousy, probably. Blind, stupid jealousy like I've never in my life felt before."

She was stunned. "You're jealous over me?"

"I've been consumed with it ever since I heard the description of the woman who slept with Barnett. So much so, I haven't been able to think straight. And then you didn't help matters today by bringing Sloan."

She leaned toward him intently. "Never mind Sloan. Once and for all let's get this one thing straightened out between us. I'm telling

you the absolute truth when I say that Richard
and I have never had an affair nor will have
one. Now do you believe me or not?"

He looked at her, his blue eyes very dark.
"I believe you. I was insanely jealous and I
tormented myself with the thought, but deep
down inside I never really let myself believe
it." He couldn't, or he would have gone truly
crazy, he thought bleakly.

Relief poured through her. "Good. Now
let's go on to the next thing, which is that I
can't tell you any more than I already have
about Richard. I will not betray the confidence of a friend, not even for you."

"Can you at least give me some indication
as to what he plans to do about the blackmail?"

"No."

"Do you know?"

She slowly shook her head in amazement.
"You won't give up, will you?"

"You do realize, don't you, that if he's
planning a cover-up, you could be cited as an
accessory because you knew and didn't tell
anyone?"

"Who and what are you most concerned
about, Matthew? Me or your story?"

In other times with other women the question would have been hard for him to answer,
but with Samantha the answer came easily.
"You. I'm worried about you."

She stared at him for several moments. It was such a simple statement, but coming from him, it took her breath away. No other man had ever been able to get past her defenses and touch her where she felt the most deeply. Her heart. But Matthew was coming perilously close. "Then trust me on this. Richard understands that his situation is very serious. He just needs some time to do what he thinks is best."

"Time? How long?"

She shook her head. "Don't ask me any more questions."

"Who's the woman he had an affair with?"

"Stop," she said softly. "Just stop."

"Then dammit, Samantha, give me something else to occupy my mind."

EIGHT

Matthew's request didn't surprise her, but her reaction did, because she didn't even have to think about it. "That sounds like a good idea," she said, lifting her hand to the V of her jacket and the first button.

He sucked in a deep breath. "Are you sure?"

"I'm sure." Since the day they had first met, desire had been building between them, growing increasingly bigger and stronger until it seemed tangible enough and monumental enough to be felt and even seen. There were issues and principles still between them, but at least they could take care of the desire right here and now. She didn't know what would happen afterward and at the moment she didn't care.

She accepted the fact that she wasn't in

control of this part of her life, the part that contained Matthew. Whenever he was around, a state of heightened alertness overcame her, and it had progressed to the point where she was now in a full-scale delirium. She wanted to make love to him as she had never wanted anything else in her life.

Matthew had the strangest feeling he was about to violate something of integral importance to him, but for the life of him he couldn't think of what it was. Did it really matter that she wouldn't tell him what he wanted to know about Barnett? Did it really matter that he couldn't always handle his feelings for her, that they seemed to pile up in him until he was ready to explode?

Like now.

She could infuriate him as easily as she could inflame him. She was definitely hazardous to his mental health, but through it all he couldn't stop wanting her.

He saw that her fingers trembled slightly as she undid the buttons one by one. She was as nervous and as anxious as he was, he reflected with satisfaction. It was only right. Their lovemaking wasn't going to be ordinary. He knew it before it had even begun.

The gold silk jacket gradually parted, and he feasted his eyes on the swell of her breasts that showed above a lace-edged, champagne-colored camisole. Her skin gleamed light

gold, the color of pale honey, and he was willing to bet she would taste sweeter and purer
than honey. Suddenly impatient, he brushed
her hand aside and finished undoing the tiny
buttons.

She looked up at him, a tentative smile on
her lips. "Something tells me I don't want to
know how you came to be so proficient at
dealing with such small buttons."

"Dexterity has never been a problem for
me."

"Nor have women, I would imagine."

"Women? What women?" He pushed the
jacket off her shoulders. It fell to the floor at
her feet, a gold puddle of silk.

"Yes," she said in soft agreement, in that
moment willing to believe just about anything
he said. "What women?"

His movements almost idle, his inner tension unbearable, he smoothed his hand across
her chest, just above the lace edge of the camisole. Her skin was the texture of velvet, yet he
knew from experience that she could be un-
yielding as steel. She was outside his experience. She kept things from him. She argued
with him. She made him mad as hell. She fascinated him. And he had the terrible feeling
he was falling hopelessly in love with her.

"Tell me Sloan is only a friend to you," he
commanded gruffly, "and make it be the
truth."

Confusion flickered in her eyes. "I've already told you that he's a friend and colleague."

"And it's the truth?"

At any other time she would have taken exception to a remark that questioned her honesty, but her pulses were racing out of control and her heart was beating like a drum, and all she could say was, "It's the truth." In a hurry to finish undressing, she kicked off her high heels. "We sometimes accompany each other to functions when we don't want to go alone but don't feel like taking a date, a *real* date."

Suddenly he untied the golden bow on her hair and slid his hands into the silky mane. Adding emphasis to what he was about to say, he curved his fingers around either side of her head and brought her close to him. "Samantha, don't ever do that to me again!"

The fierceness of the demand caught her off guard. "Do what?"

"Seeing you with him this afternoon made me absolutely crazy! I was miserable."

And then she understood. Her expression was solemn as she gazed at him. "I'm sorry. You were right about what I was doing, by the way. I was trying to use him as a shield between you and me. It wasn't fair to either of you."

"And in the end it didn't do a damned bit

of good." He bit out the words. "Because now I'm going to make you mine."

There was no misunderstanding his statement. It was bald and unadorned, and something very basic and feminine inside her thrilled to it. But her reaction was nothing compared with what happened when he brought his mouth down on hers. . . .

She went up in flames.

Time stopped, the surroundings faded, any doubts she had quieted. She became immersed in his taste, in his touch, in his smell. He made her hungry for him, greedy, and she was amazed at herself.

A terrible urgency gripped her, pushing her to explore him, to discover the different textures and tastes of his body, to learn what excited him, what electrified him, what turned him inside out and made him incoherent with need for her.

But could she really do that? She wasn't sure she had the power. It was all totally unlike her, but at this moment their relationship had dissolved to something very elemental where only the most primitive of sensations and emotions mattered. There was nothing she wouldn't do for him, and she couldn't wait to show him.

"*God*, what is it about you?" he exclaimed, his mouth against hers. "I can't stop kissing you."

She didn't want him to, but if they didn't move into the bedroom soon, she was going to sink to the floor and beg him to take her there. Some romantic part of her wanted their first time to be in her bed, though. After all, their first time might be their last.

She pulled back and drew in a great, gulping breath. "Come with me."

"Right now," he growled, "you could lead me to hell, and as long as it's not too far, I'd follow."

"It's not hell and it's not far."

But they hadn't gone but a few feet when he stopped her again, twirling her into his arms and kissing her. "It's too far," he muttered against her mouth. "I can't wait."

"Wait," she said, her voice a mere breath.

They walked, they caressed, they kissed. And somewhere along the way her skirt and camisole came off, as did his jacket and shirt.

They were in a fever, groping and fumbling with their clothes, but always coming back to the other's body. She found she couldn't keep her hands off him. His skin was smooth and hot, and beneath it strong muscles moved and shifted. Somehow her bra and panties disappeared. Making love to Matthew had become as necessary to her as breathing, and she was quivering with anticipation, hardly able to wait.

Inside the bedroom door he impatiently

lifted her into his arms and carried her the rest of the way to the bed. She sank down into the ivory-colored down comforter, and after he had finished undressing, he followed.

Shimmering gold thigh-high hose were all that remained on her. When she started to push them down her legs, he stopped her.

"No. Leave them for now." His gaze traveled the length of her body. "You look sexy as hell in them."

Just for a moment she was embarrassed, and then the moment passed. Her body was demanding satisfaction, and when he took one breast into his hand and his mouth closed around the rigid nipple, her stomach contracted and her hips lifted in an undulating motion, and she cried out in pleasure.

He suckled strongly, tasting her flavor, inhaling the scent of her heated skin. He wasn't going to be able to wait much longer to get inside her, he realized. But he wanted to. As smart and as tough as she could be at times, she was also delicate and fragile. He didn't want to hurt her. This lovemaking should be prolonged, savored—for her sake, for his sake.

His hand skimmed over her skin, down her stomach, to between her thighs. There moistness awaited him. His fingers probed and discovered the tiny nub that would give her the ultimate ecstasy.

He gently stroked, and waves of pleasure

washed through her. She felt as if she were being swept along by a powerful riptide of heat and there was an immediate need to get to her destination.

She tugged at his arm and whispered, "Make love to me."

He didn't need any more urging. He was so hard, he felt as though he were going to explode. Gazing down at her, he saw Samantha on fire with passion for him, and it excited him beyond belief. Her skin was flushed and her eyes were half closed as if, he thought with satisfaction, she had stopped seeing and was only feeling. Her chest rose and fell with the exertion of her breathing. Her breasts were firm, her nipples puckered and still wet from his mouth. "I'll be more than happy to."

He moved over her and began to enter her a little at a time. He felt her muscles stretch to accommodate him, then close tightly around him. By the time he was buried completely inside her, he was shuddering with the effort of holding back, and a thin sheen of sweat covered his skin.

He began slowly stroking in and out, but she wasn't interested in slow. She wrapped her legs around his hips and skimmed her hands down his back to his buttocks. "Please," she whispered urgently.

Her stockings felt like textured silk against his skin. In fact being inside her was like being gripped by hot, erotically textured silk. It was wildly exciting. He pulled his hips back and surged into her, drawing a gasp of ecstasy from her. He covered her mouth with his and began moving quicker and faster and driving deeper into her. He knew exactly what he was doing, heading toward the crest of ecstasy and taking her with him.

Sobbing, she bucked and twisted beneath him, digging her fingers into his back. With anyone else she would not have felt safe enough to let go as she was doing. But Matthew was in complete control of her body and she had never felt safer. It didn't make sense, but she couldn't think about it now.

Pure, unadulterated need gripped her body, a need so powerful and so raw, it was consuming her, burning her alive. Matthew was her salvation, and softly she pleaded with him to help her. She hoped he heard her, she prayed he did, because she didn't think she could help herself.

He was an expert when it came to making love to her body. How had that happened? she wondered vaguely. He didn't simply use power, something he had plenty of, but he used finesse and knowledge and an uncanny instinct.

Each time he drove into her, he took her that much closer to climax. The pleasure became more excruciating, more unbearable, more exciting. And then the end came and the beginning started. She stiffened as a white-hot haze of pleasure gripped her and sent her soaring.

Feeling the contractions of her release, he let himself go, thrusting into her, joining her, soaring with her.

Samantha came slowly awake, and as she did so, she became aware of several things at once. It was night, she was naked, and she was alone.

She wasn't used to a man being beside her when she waked, but she had known immediately that Matthew was gone and she missed him acutely. She pushed her hair from her face and levered herself up in bed, bringing the covers with her. As an afterthought she leaned over and turned on the bedside lamp.

Antique furniture she had spent hours refinishing filled the room. Ivory lace curtains hung at the windows, puffed here and there and tied with gold, yellow, and apricot-colored ribbons. An ivory, down-filled comforter covered the big brass bed and her. It was a warm, inviting room and, except for her, empty, completely empty.

Well, great, she thought. *Just great*. Matthew had gotten the sex he wanted from her and then left as she slept.

She settled back against the pillows, closed her eyes, and tried to decide how she felt. The sex, she had to admit, had been fabulous. Their coming together had been as powerful as if they had made love hundreds of times before, and yet it had been fresh and new, a discovery of what was possible, what could be. She had been left drained and exhausted and had fallen asleep in his arms. And then he had left.

Something deep in her chest hurt, and she remembered thinking hours before how he was able to reach past her defenses and touch her heart. Was that what had happened? Had her heart somehow become involved?

With a groan she rolled over and buried her face in the pillows. She should have known better. She could match other people up with the right person, but not herself. She should have kept going through her address book until she found exactly the right person for him, someone with a bad overbite and even worse skin. She groaned again, this time at herself.

"What's the matter?" a deep voice asked.

Startled, she rolled over onto her back to see Matthew, standing in the doorway, a concerned look on his face. He was wearing his dark-blue trousers, but his feet and chest were bare, and in his hands he carried a tray. *He hadn't left after all.*

"I heard you groan. Are you feeling bad? Do you hurt? Did *I* hurt you?" As he talked, he crossed the room, rounded the bed, and sat down beside her.

Recovering from her surprise, she scrambled toward the center of the bed to give him more room to sit, careful all the while to hold the sheet against her. "No, I'm fine."

He balanced the tray on his lap. "Are you sure? You don't need an aspirin or something?"

"No, really, I don't need anything." She paused. "I thought you had left."

"Ah." He nodded understandingly. "You woke up alone and immediately jumped to the conclusion that I was the kind of man who would make love to a woman and then leave without so much as a good-bye."

She shrugged, she hoped nonchalantly. "That's what it looked like had happened."

"And it bothered you?"

"No woman likes to feel incidental."

His hand shot out to cup the back of her neck and bring her to him for a long, deep kiss that sent fire to the pit of her stomach and then lower into her loins and the insides of her thighs. By the time he pulled away, she was clinging to him, and the sheet had fallen to her waist.

The newly kindled desire had darkened the color of his eyes and had turned his voice soft and husky as he asked, "Did that kiss make you feel that I in any way consider you incidental?"

"It made me feel that you still want me."

"Guess what? That's because I do. But I'm positive there's nothing new about that thought. I've wanted you from the beginning, and now that we've made love, I still want you." He smiled at her. "And as you can see, I didn't leave, as you thought. Now, unless you *want* me to leave . . . ?"

"No."

"Good." His smile broadened, and his eyes dropped to her breasts and their golden-brown peaks that were still rigid, a sign of the effect his kiss had had on her. Unable to resist, he bent his head and took one peak into his mouth, twirling his tongue around the nipple, then lightly nipping.

She softly moaned as new heat surged through her.

"Good," he said again, raising his head, "because I brought sustenance." He lifted the tray and placed it over her lap. "I'm no cook, but I can put stuff together."

The desire she saw in his eyes matched exactly what she was feeling inside. It made her want to tell him to forget food and make love to her again. But making love to him was all so new. She felt as if the world had tilted off its axis and she wanted to right it again before anything else happened between them.

She cleared her throat, wishing she could as easily clear her body of the need for him. Belatedly she remembered to pull the sheet up, bring it over her breasts, and secure it beneath her arms. And where were her hose? she wondered.

They had just spent the last couple of hours in the most intimate way two people could, but his gaze had spread a rosy hue of embarrassment over her skin. She forced her attention to the tray.

The tray held a plate of Brie, blue, and herb cheeses, thick slices of her homemade baked bread, and two small bowls filled with grapes, sliced strawberries, and bananas. In addition there were two glasses of strawberry wine. She was hungry only for him, but she said, "It's very nice."

He picked up one glass, handed her the other, then clinked the rim of his against the one she was holding. "To your wine and to you. Your wine is remarkable, but you are far and away more intoxicating."

Doubts niggled at her about Matthew and the wisdom of continuing whatever they had started. But she was very, very happy he had stayed, and no matter what else happened, it was intensely gratifying to be wanted by him.

For the first time since she had awakened, she smiled. "That's quite a toast."

"It came easily because it's the truth." He waved a hand toward the tray. "Eat. The night isn't over yet, and you're going to need your strength."

Because it was exactly what she wanted to hear, she was completely unnerved. "You sound pretty sure of yourself." She picked up a grape and popped it into her mouth.

He grinned. "*Hopeful* is the word I would use."

"And once the night *is* over?"

His forehead lined. "You mean tomorrow? Sunday?"

"Yes."

He eyed her thoughtfully. "I can't decide if you want me to say 'I'll go home tomorrow first thing in the morning and leave you alone' or if you want me to say 'I'll stay.' "

She chewed on another grape. "To tell you the truth, I don't know either."

"I'd rather you say you'd like me to stay." When she remained silent, his expression turned serious, and he leaned toward her. "Hey . . . whatever happens, this is not going to be a one-night stand, at least it won't be if I can help it. Is that what you're worried about? That this will be a one-night stand?"

She stared at him for several moments. It might last for more than one night, but it wasn't going to last forever. The two of them were like two pieces of flint. Matthew was interested in her because of the knowledge she had about Richard and because of the fire they could make together. But one way or the other the story would soon be over, and a fire always died down. Besides, Matthew wasn't the type of man to fall in love with a woman so hard that he would want to spend the rest of his life with her. He might devote a few weeks or even a few months to a story, but in the end he always moved on to the next story, and he would be that way with a woman too.

"Actually I was wondering something else. I was wondering if you had slept with me to get information about Richard."

With a violent curse he lurched off the bed. "Of all the dumb, stupid, idiotic, asinine things to think, Samantha, that really takes the cake!"

"Gee, Matthew, why don't you tell me how you really feel."

"How could you even *think* such a thing?"

She set the tray to one side. "If you'll think back a few hours, you'll realize it wasn't that far a mental leap for me to take. You were grilling me about Richard right up until the moment we decided to make love, and I'm sure you wouldn't be the first journalist to go to bed with someone in the hopes of getting inside information on a story."

He smacked his forehead with the palm of his hand. "Oh, that's right," he said, his tone dripping with sarcasm. "How could I have forgotten in what high regard you hold the members of my profession? Worms-journalists, journalists-worms. It's all the same to you, isn't it?"

She exhaled a long breath. "Maybe this was all a mistake. Maybe you *should* go home now."

Matthew planted his hands on his hips. "There you go again, sending me home, but I'm not going this time, at least not right now. There's something here I don't think you've considered. I could just as easily turn the table on you and say that I was wondering if you'd gone to bed with me in order to divert my attention away from your great and good friend the judge. And if you did do that, I've got to admit it's a hell of a ploy. While we were making love, I didn't once think of Barnett or the upcoming Tate trial."

She came away from the pillows, her back ramrod straight. "You can't believe that!"

"Why not? If you can, why can't I."

"Because it's not the *truth*."

He pointed a finger at her. "Bingo."

Her eyes narrowed. "You think you've got me, don't you?"

"I'm working on it."

She rubbed her eyes, then looked away

again. She had always kept her personal life calm and free of conflict, but since she had met Matthew, she had known nothing but a turmoil of highs and lows. It had kept her off balance, something she hated.

"Truce, Samantha?" When she remained silent, he said, "Samantha, look at me." He returned to the bed and her side. "Look at me," he commanded softly, and with a finger beneath her chin turned her face so that he could see her eyes. "Do you really believe I made love to you to get information from you?"

Maybe not, but he hadn't said one word about being in love with her.

The sudden thought took her totally by surprise. Was *that* what was worrying her? How very, very foolish of her. "I'm not sure." She was confused about a lot of things, she realized.

Obviously disappointed, he dropped his hand from her face. "Do you really believe I'm that kind of man, and do you really believe I think that simply by sleeping with you you'll tell me something you might not have said otherwise?"

She slid out of bed and went to her closet for a robe. "Tough questions, Matthew. Complicated answers."

He eyed her slender body, naked and sleek with womanly curves that made his mouth go dry. After the hours they had just spent together he would have thought he would be sated, but it wasn't the case. Even now hard knots of need were forming in his stomach. Would he ever stop wanting her? He didn't think so.

Before they made love, he remembered having the terrible feeling that he might be falling in love with her. Now it was no longer simply a feeling. It was a fact. He was falling fast and hard, and there was nothing he could do to stop himself, nor did he want to. "The questions sound simple to me."

With jerky movements she belted the robe around her. "Think about it, Matthew. We've had an adversarial relationship since we first met."

"That was my fault. I jumped to conclusions about Alfred and blamed it on you."

"And when that was cleared up to your satisfaction, the story about Richard came up."

He shifted until he was lying against the pillows, his long legs stretched out over the ivory comforter. "Okay, there's friction between us. But it looks to me as if we've both survived it pretty well, and look at the heat the friction between us produces."

She gazed at him, feeling somewhat bemused. He appeared completely at home and set to stay. "Right, it produces great chemistry."

"The chemistry's been there since the first," he said, agreeing.

"But what else?"

"Stimulating conversation." He chuckled. "Come on, you have to admit it. We're never bored around each other. Besides, look on the bright side of things. Sooner or later we're bound to run out of conflicts."

"And when that happens? Matthew, you and I have been guarded with each other since the first."

"Yeah, but it seemed to me that what just happened in this bed stripped away those guards, at least some of them. I wish I knew exactly what was bothering you." He patted the bed. "Come over here and tell me what I can do to fix it."

She felt foolish. She was asking for assurances about a relationship that was in its infant stages. There were no assurances he could give her that would make any impact on her. There were no certainties, no guarantees. *And since when did she need any?*

"Samantha?"

Flipping her hair free of the robe's collar, she walked slowly to him and sat down on the edge of the mattress beside him. "I'm sorry. Just forget everything I've said."

"No, you wouldn't have said anything unless you were worried, and you're right."

"I am?"

He lightly brushed his fingers over her hair. He loved the feel of her hair, her skin. In fact, he thought, he hadn't found anything he didn't love about her. He smiled. "I'll tell you what—make a deal with me."

"A deal?"

"Let's take the rest of this weekend just for ourselves and shut out the rest of the world."

The thought sent excitement streaming through her veins. "Really?"

"Yeah, but there's a catch."

Her excitement faded. She might have known that with Matthew there would always be a catch. "What?"

"To shut out the rest of the world, we'll have to turn off our beepers."

"My beeper is always turned off on the weekends."

His smile broadened. "I should have guessed that. Compartmentalization. Nothing of your work touches your personal life."

"Sometimes it does, but not often. But you live your life differently. Your work *is* your life."

"To a certain extent."

"And *you'd* be willing to turn off your beeper?"

He was surprised himself. His beeper was

the only way anyone could reach him this weekend. The newspaper, his contacts—no one knew he was with Samantha. And if something important came up and Gates wanted to get hold of him, he wouldn't be able to. But the impulse to turn it off wouldn't go away. "I'd be willing to and more than that. We could ban newspapers and television news shows."

"But what will we do?"

His eyes began to twinkle. "I'm confident we'll find something."

Her lips quirked. "Besides *that.*"

"I don't know what we'll do exactly, but I think it'll be interesting to find out, don't you?"

Yes, she thought, she did.

"How else are we going to find out if we genuinely have a problem getting along or if our conflicts up to now have been caused by the situations we've found ourselves in?"

Her gaze was thoughtful. "Why are you doing this?"

"Believe it or not, I think a weekend with you would be fun."

She finally smiled. "Then I think it's a great idea."

NINE

They made love again. They were still too hungry for each other not to. They couldn't *not* reach out for each other. The burning was too hot, the intensity too strong. And so they found themselves coming together time and again throughout the night. But in between they also did other things. . . .

"What time is it?" Samantha asked Matthew drowsily.

"Time?" His mouth was near her ear, his naked body spooned around hers. "I haven't got the faintest idea. Why?"

"I'm hungry and I don't remember eating."

"I don't either. Not food anyway."

Pleasure shivered through her as she recalled their last bout of lovemaking. She didn't think there was a patch of skin on her body he hadn't kissed, licked, or fondled. Would it be possible to go back to her regular life after tonight was over? A life without Matthew, a life without touches from his deft hands and kisses from his skilled mouth and clever tongue?

Unfortunately the answer was painfully clear and simple. She would have to.

"I was thinking about food," she finally said.

"Why?"

He lifted his head and pressed his mouth to her ear, a short, light kiss that produced a massive quake of emotions inside her.

She opened her eyes and glanced at her bedside clock. It was nearly midnight. "Because unlike you who can obviously exist on air—"

"Or you. I can exist on you very well."

She couldn't help but smile. "Right. Well, as I was saying, unlike you, I do need the occasional sandwich or bowl of soup to keep me going."

"You're enough for me, but I'm not enough for you? If I had the energy, I might get my feelings hurt. But since I don't . . ." He stirred, raising up on one elbow. "What happened to the tray I brought in?"

"I can't remember."

"Then I say we forget it." He lay back

down, slid his arm around her waist, and drew her closer against him.

With a small giggle she rolled over to face him. "What are you running on? Batteries?"

"Yeah, the long-lasting kind." He slid his hand down her side to her bottom, cupped his hand around its firm roundness, and pulled her against his hardening groin, showing her he would soon be ready for her again.

She gave a mental groan as she realized how easy it would be for him to draw her back down into the whirlpool of passion. "Protein," she said with determination. "We both need protein. It will give us energy."

"Get energy so that I could have my feelings hurt?" He nuzzled his lips in the softness of her neck. "I don't think so. Why would I want to do that?"

"Never mind." With another giggle she rolled away from him and peered over the edge of the bed to the floor. "Here's the tray." She looked it over. "Would you like bread, cheese, and fruit served at room temperature?"

"Sounds good. Or at least at one time I seem to recall I *thought* it sounded good. What's your call on it?"

She lifted the tray to the bed and placed it between them. "I say any port in a storm. We need fuel, and this"—she waved her hand toward the tray—"is fuel. And as an added bo-

nus the Brie is sufficiently softened so that
we'll have no problem spreading it."

Without bothering to pull a sheet over his
nakedness, he sat up in bed and stuffed a pillow behind his head. "Are you all right? I
mean . . ."

She grinned wryly. "You mean, how am I
surviving the physicality of the evening?"

His grin was as wry as hers. "That was
very delicately put and exactly what I meant.
Are you getting sore?" He tenderly caressed
her cheek with the back of his hand. "Should I
tell my body enough is enough?"

The question implied that he had more
lovemaking in mind. As the hours went by,
their need for each other was growing instead
of abating, and she was thrilled by the fact. It
wouldn't last of course. Soon they would become sated, and when that happened, they
would grow tired of each other and become
anxious to return to the private spaces of their
own individual lives. But they had promised
each other the rest of the weekend, and she
for one planned to enjoy every moment that
remained.

"I'm great, just great," she said. And she
was, physically at least. But emotionally she
didn't feel at all like herself. She felt as if in
the past hours she had come unraveled, un-
done.

"Not even a little bit tired?"

"I guess I should be, but I'm not."

"Me either." With a smile he popped a cube of cheese into his mouth.

"Help yourself," she said, sliding quickly off the bed. "I'll be right back."

"Wait," he said clearly disconcerted. "Where are you going?"

"The bathroom. I'll be right back," she said again, disappearing into the next room. Alone, she washed up, ran a comb through her hair, and donned her robe. Then, feeling a bit more together, she returned to the bedroom, vowing that she would shower after she had eaten.

"Do you have a television in here?" he asked.

"Sure do." She pointed toward the antique armoire positioned against the wall opposite from the bed. "There's a VCR, too, and I have quite a few tapes."

He nodded. "I don't watch much TV, but occasionally I'll watch a movie. What do you have?"

"Why don't you look for yourself?" She arranged several pillows against the headboard, then sat down beside him. "Maybe you could find something you like."

"I'll do that. But in the meantime how would you like me to make you an omelet?"

Her eyebrows lifted. "I thought you said you couldn't cook."

"I can't, but I can make something that *resembles* an omelet, and most of the time it doesn't taste too bad either."

"A typical bachelor."

His eyes twinkled with laughter. "Don't sneer. I could learn to cook if I wanted to. It's just that it's more convenient to eat out."

"Do you even *own* a set of pots and pans?" She surveyed the tray, then opted for herb cheese spread on a slice of a bread. She had eaten several bites before she realized he hadn't answered her question. She was reaching for a wineglass when she glanced at him and saw a pensive expression on his face. "Matthew?"

"I have a set of pots and pans. My wife and I received them as wedding gifts."

Carefully she set the wineglass down. "Your *wife?*"

He nodded. "I was married for eighteen months."

"You *were* married?" The words felt as if they were strangling her.

"That's right. I married a wonderful girl I met in college our junior year. Her name was Melissa, and we married one month to the day after we graduated from college. She was a journalism major like me." He gazed toward the end of the bed as he spoke, but his sight was directed inward. Instead of the ivory comforter he was seeing the laughing green eyes of the woman he had once loved. "She would have been a great reporter. She was extremely talented and bright."

The shock was clearing from her mind. "You're speaking in the past tense. Why?"

"She had leukemia. In fact she had it when we married, but she was convinced she was in remission. Maybe she truly was, or maybe she simply wanted very badly to believe she was in remission. At any rate she didn't tell me about her illness until after we married and she started to have symptoms again."

"You mean you married her without knowing she had leukemia?"

For the first time he looked at Samantha. "It wouldn't have made any difference. I would have married her anyway. I was very much in love with her. But I would have liked to have known. Maybe I could have helped in some way, even if it was only to bear some of the burden of worry." His shrug held a touch of helplessness. "I don't know. I wish she had trusted me enough to tell me the truth, but I did the best I could for her until the end."

Filled with compassion for him, she reached out and covered his hand with hers. "Maybe she didn't tell you because she wanted to spare you."

He rubbed a hand over his face. "That's what she said later during the last few days we had together, but then that's not what love is supposed to be about, is it? Isn't it supposed to be about sharing and trusting and helping each other?"

She couldn't bear the thought of the pain he must have gone through. He had been so young, he must have been overwhelmed with grief. The very fact that Leona had never mentioned Melissa to her told her that his wounds had been very deep. She had the wild urge to make it up to him in some way, but the urge was unrealistic. No one could make up to him the death of his young bride. He had loved Melissa enough to plan a future with her, maybe even a family, and make her his wife. Then he had had to watch her die.

Not so long ago she had reflected that he wasn't the type of man to fall in love with a woman so hard that he would want to spend the rest of his life with her. It had been her opinion that he would always move on to the next story, the next woman, and she had been right. It was how he was today. But now she knew he hadn't always been that way. Once he had been young and unguarded, and she wished with everything that was in her that she had known him then.

"I'm afraid I'm not an expert on love, but your definition sounds right to me."

A small smile touched his lips as he studied her, his eyes enigmatic. "I'm no expert either, but I did love her very much. I would have done anything for her."

"I'm so very sorry, Matthew."

He squeezed her hand. "I am too. Melissa will always have a special place in my heart, but in case you're wondering, I'm completely over both her and her death. She died thirteen years ago."

She considered him thoughtfully. "You don't tell many people about Melissa, do you?"

"No."

"I appreciate your telling me."

He took her hand, brought it to his mouth, and pressed a kiss to its back. "I thought you should know."

Why? she wondered. Was he warning her? Was it his way of explaining to her not to expect too much from him? His marriage had ended in sorrow, and because of it she could certainly understand why he wouldn't want to commit to a woman again.

"I'll go brew us a fresh pot of coffee," she said, her heart feeling strangely heavy.

Matthew looked around as Samantha returned from having just showered. She was wearing the ivory satin robe again, and even from the distance of several feet he could smell the perfumed soap she had used. The scent was faintly floral, faintly spice. He knew because when he had showered minutes before, he had picked up the bar of soap and taken a whiff. Her bathroom was filled with all kinds of soaps and oils, feminine paraphernalia designed to boggle a man's mind. All he knew was that he liked the results. For himself he had finally settled on a naturally milled, unscented bar of soap.

He hadn't wanted to shower alone, he remembered, but she had slipped off the bed and disappeared into the kitchen. He supposed he couldn't complain too much since when he got out of the shower, he had found a freshly laid tray of assorted food, including two slices of apple pie topped with ice cream. While he had eaten, she had decided to shower.

It was the *last* thing they would do apart this weekend, he decided.

He turned his attention back to the television and pressed his finger to the remote control. "I can't find anything that looks good."

Samantha settled onto the bed beside him. He had a towel wrapped around his waist. After the hours they had just spent together she supposed she should be used to seeing him without clothes. But she still experienced a certain electrical thrill when she looked at him and saw his lean bare torso with soft coppery brown hair curling across his chest and covering his muscled legs.

She felt as if she were in the eye of a hurricane. She knew the lull was only temporary. Soon the turmoil would return—their lives, their conflicts—and when it did, she would have to consider the consequences of throwing rational thought and caution to the winds for the weekend. For now, though, she was content and happy. "I haven't got the faintest idea what television on Saturday night is like, especially this late. I guess technically it's really Sunday morning, isn't it. If I'm home, I usually read or rent a movie." She finished off the last bit of apple pie on her dessert plate, then licked her fingers.

He glanced at her fingers and then her mouth. "*If* you're home? Does that mean you go out a lot?"

"I've already told you I date occasionally, but I also told you that my matchmaking abilities don't extend to myself. I usually go out with friends, and then there's the inevitable function I'm required for one reason or another to attend."

"The ones where you and Sloan go together?"

"That's right."

"It must be a lawyer thing, because I don't have to go to that many 'functions,' as you call them."

"Thank your lucky stars. They're usually very boring." She paused. "I could ask you if you go out a lot, but to tell you the truth, I don't really want to know."

He tossed the remote control aside. "Why not?"

Because of the hours they had just spent together, his question required honesty. Besides, in this case the honest answer had to be painfully apparent to him. "That's simple. I've just spent the evening making love with you, and at this particular moment I don't think I would enjoy thinking of you with another woman. Jealousy isn't exclusive to men, you know."

"No kidding?"

Her lips twisted ruefully. "No kidding. And try not to sound so pleased."

"Sorry, but it only seems fair after the afternoon I spent at Aunt Leona's wedding. But Samantha"—his voice lowered and turned gentle—"I can't even remember the last *date* I had, and the last woman I kissed and made love to was you. You've pushed everyone else out of my mind."

Emotion threatened to close her throat. "That was a terrific answer. I really liked it."

He lifted her hand to his mouth and kissed her palm. "Good, because it's the truth."

She cleared her throat and looked away. "Have you given up on television?"

"Yeah. You said you had tapes?"

She waved her hand toward the armoire. "Yeah, I have some good ones. They're in the bottom two drawers."

He slid off the bed and went to investigate, a faint smile on his face. "Seeing what kind of movies you like is going to be interesting. Your definition of good is probably entirely different from mine."

"You think so? Okay—before you open the drawers, tell me what kind you think I like."

With a grin he sat down on the floor and crossed his legs. "Courtroom dramas or movies about lawyers. *Kramer versus Kramer*, for instance. And *To Kill a Mockingbird*. Or more recently *The Firm*."

The sight of his crossed legs parting the edges of the towel made it hard for her to keep her mind on movies. "You're going for the obvious, Matthew. I'm deeply disappointed in you. It would be the same as my guessing that you liked stories that have something to do with newspapers. *Citizen Kane* and *All the President's Men*, for instance. It's almost cheating."

"I disagree, because as a matter of fact I do like both of them. *Citizen Kane* is a classic, and *All the President's Men* was great because it was true."

She airily waved her hand. "As I said—

cheating. It's almost a given that you would favor those types of movies. Take another guess about what you think is in those drawers."

"Okay, let's see. You probably have Martha Stewart tapes—lots of them. Gardening, decorating, cooking . . ."

She groaned good-naturedly. "You're not even warm. In fact you're somewhere in the region of the Arctic Circle, but never mind. Just look and see if you can find anything you think you might want to see."

He opened the drawers and began pulling out tapes. *"Lethal Weapon?"* He looked at her in surprise. "You have *Lethal Weapon?"*

She nodded, her expression smug. "Not only the original but Two *and* Three. See? You don't know so much."

His eyes narrowed skeptically on her. "Those are action movies. Are you trying to tell me you actually like action movies?"

"Uh-huh." She grinned. "I also like Mel Gibson. A *lot*. He's got great blue eyes . . . among other things."

"What other things?"

"Remember that opening shot in the original *Lethal Weapon?* There was a great shot of his backside."

His eyes narrowed. "So you've got a thing for Mel Gibson's backside, huh?"

He didn't sound very pleased.

She grinned. "Like I said, among other things." She was enjoying their exchange. Up to now—and excluding the time during which they had made love—they had usually been at each other's throats. It felt good to tease and talk about nonsensical things. "I don't exactly have a crush on the man, but I do happen to enjoy a great pair of blue eyes . . . along with certain other parts of the anatomy."

He looked at her blankly. "I don't get it. What do blue eyes and a great butt have to do with a cop-buddy film?"

"For some women just about everything." She laughed at his obvious puzzlement, but also because in her estimation his blue eyes and backside rivaled those of Mel Gibson's any day. In fact they were better, because Mel Gibson had never made her weak in the knees with just a look in her direction, nor had his eyes ever grown dark with need just before he kissed and made love to her. "I suppose you've been laboring under the misapprehension that it's the car chases and the buildings that are blown up that make people line up to buy those tickets."

"It's why I line up."

"Well, next time you're standing in one of those lines, look around you. At least half the people in the line will be women." She slid off the bed and reached for the tray. "Do you want anything from the kitchen?"

He gazed up at her. "Weren't you just in the kitchen?"

She smiled, slightly puzzled at his question. "No, I was in the shower. Before that I was in the kitchen. Why?"

"Nothing. I just get lonely when you're gone. Hurry back."

Oh, yes, she thought, his blue eyes were far better than Mel Gibson's.

When she returned, she found half her tapes on the floor. "I put some coffee on. Have you found anything you want to watch?"

"Yeah, I've found several." He held one up. "You like *Dirty Harry*?"

"I've always liked the way Clint Eastwood squints."

He looked appalled. "You're kidding. *That's* why you have the movie?"

She burst out laughing. "What difference does it make why I like a movie or why you like it? As long as we both find something in it to enjoy, we can have a great time watching it together."

"I guess you're right." He sorted through a few tapes, then brought one up. "Here's one." He slipped it into the VCR, then joined her on the bed.

She watched the television screen curiously as music started up and then the title appeared. "A Fred Astaire–Ginger Rogers movie? You *like* Fred Astaire–Ginger Rogers movies?"

"I never have before," he said, reaching for her. "But I'm willing to bet Cole Porter music is great to make love to."

She chuckled softly and slid her arms around his neck. "You see what I mean? What difference does it make why we like a movie as long as we can enjoy it together?"

"I see what you mean," he said huskily, and lowered his mouth to hers for a long, hot kiss that was only a prelude to more long, hot kisses.

Samantha moved drowsily and found herself held tightly against Matthew, cradled in the crook of his arm, her face resting on his chest. Beneath her cheek she could hear the slow, steady beating of his heart. Through the lace curtains she could see that it was already morning.

Several movies had run through the VCR last night. A couple of them, she recalled with a faint smile, they had even watched. And she had been surprised at how much fun it had been. They had rehashed each plot, dissected each character. They had even recited classic lines of dialogue to each other.

"What are you smiling at?" Matthew asked sleepily.

She tilted her head so that she could see
him. "How did you know I was smiling?"

"I felt your cheek move and your mouth
curve."

"You're pretty sharp."

"Yep."

"Then maybe you can tell me what day it
is."

He chuckled, and she listened to the sound
rumbling in his chest. It was a nice sound, she
concluded. A somehow reassuring sound.

"We've managed to pack so many great
things into such a small amount of time that it
seems like Sunday of next week, but I'm afraid
it's Sunday of this week."

"Why *afraid*?"

"Because our weekend alone together is
drawing to a close. We have only today left."

She considered that. "Does that mean
you'll be leaving tonight? Or will you spend
the night?"

He looked down at her. "I hadn't given it
too much thought. What would you prefer?"

"Maybe we should wait and see how today
goes. By tonight we could be arguing again."

"Or, as you put it to Sloan, we could be
having a discussion with two different points
of view."

She shrugged. "You know, Matthew, disagreements aren't always bad. My parents
never disagreed or argued, but they had a mis-

erable marriage. Maybe if they had disagreed more, it would have been better for them. If they had talked things out and learned to respect the other's opinion, they might have been happier."

"You mean if they could have agreed to disagree?"

"Something like that. At least they would have gotten off their chest what was bothering them instead of holding everything in."

"Well, I don't think anyone could accuse us of holding in what's bothering us."

"That's certainly true." She chuckled. "But it's been fairly easy to argue with you since you've been in the wrong right from the beginning."

He sat straight up and glared at her, but his eyes were glinting with humor. "In exactly *whose* opinion?"

An impish grin on her face, she pointed to herself. "In *my* opinion, and after all, it's my opinion that counts."

He grabbed a pillow and lightly whacked her with it. "You think so, do you?"

She laughed. "Yes, I do. And I'm always right."

"*Except* when you're arguing with me."

She shook her head. "No, I'm sorry, but there are no exceptions."

His eyes narrowed playfully. "I think

you've got a lot to learn. It's a good thing the weekend isn't over yet."

"And who do you think is going to teach me?"

"What the hell. I'll give it a go. And if I can't teach you to give my viewpoints their proper respect, homage, and awe, then—"

"*Homage and awe?* No one said anything about homage and awe."

"*I* did. Weren't you listening? And as I was saying, if I can't teach you, then I'll just have to wash my hands of you and write you off as unteachable, not to mention wrong."

She made a mock sound of fury. "Did anyone ever tell you that you're insufferable?"

He grinned. "Insufferable? Many times, but no one as pretty as you ever has. And you know what? Call me crazy, but telling me I'm insufferable somehow doesn't smack of respect. That's not good, Samantha."

"Smack? I'll give you a smack." She bopped him over the head with a pillow.

Laughing, he held his hands over his head. "Okay, *okay*! I give up."

"That's what I like to hear. Total surrender."

Quick as lightning he wrapped his fingers around her upper arms and pulled her across the bed to him. "Well, not *total* surrender. Just partial. Remember, I've had some sleep. My batteries are recharged."

She should have been tired of him. During this weekend she had made love to this one man more than she had made love in her entire life. And still her body hungered for him. "Would you please tell me the name of the batteries you use? I'd like to buy stock in them."

"Sorry, I have exclusive rights. The only way you can get any benefits from them is if you keep me around."

"I'll take it under advisement."

"I just love it when you talk lawyer."

She grinned. "Shut up and kiss me."

"Yes, ma'am," he said reaching for her. "I'm happy to oblige."

Matthew made his way through Samantha's house, picking up an item here and there, studying it, then putting it down. He could hear Samantha in the kitchen moving around. Occasionally he would hear the clink of a pot or the rattle of a dish. He liked the sound.

He couldn't remember when he had spent this much time off from work. He didn't like vacations, even short ones. He had never been able to find anything to do that kept him as entertained and as interested as running down a story. That's why he was amazed at how contented he was now. Doing nothing with Samantha. Doing everything.

He made his way into the kitchen to find her standing at the stove, barefoot in jeans and a T-shirt. The mere sight of her enchanted him. He was in love with her and he didn't know what to do about it. How would she take the news when he told her? His inclination was to tell her, then demand that she love him in return. Unfortunately he knew that wouldn't work. And he was so afraid that when he finally told her, she would smile at him with compassion and then politely but firmly tell him their relationship and their weekend was over.

"What are you doing?"

"I decided to make a quick batch of vegetable soup."

He frowned. "What's quick about vegetable soup?"

"The way I'm doing it is. I had just about everything in the freezer. The stock and most of the vegetables. I've just had to chop a few additional things. It won't be too much longer." He was wearing his trousers and T-shirt. It was a very masculine combination, she reflected, but then she hadn't seen him in anything yet that hadn't stirred her blood. "Are you hungry?"

"I could eat something," he admitted,

crossing to the stove and gazing down into the pot. "It smells good."

"It will be good. Are you getting cabin fever?"

He grinned. "Maybe *Samantha* fever."

"You know what I mean. We haven't been out of the house since yesterday afternoon. That's not unusual for me on a weekend, but I would guess it is for you."

"Well, you have to understand, my house isn't as comfortable and homelike as yours is, although I never thought about it too much before I spent time here."

"You never knew your home wasn't comfortable?"

He perched on the stool beside the butcher-block table. "I use it to sleep, change clothes, and sometimes eat. Otherwise I'm someplace else."

She eyed him thoughtfully. "I guess a home is more important to some people than it is to others."

"It's obviously important to you. Has it always been like that? I mean, did you start out with a dollhouse, hooking little rugs and making tiny curtains?"

A wry smile curved her lips. "As a matter of fact I did. I had the best-decorated dollhouse on my block."

He chuckled. "I bet you did. Did your mother teach you how to do all that stuff?"

"No. Most of it I picked up on my own."
Her smile faded. "I turned my dollhouse and
later this house into what I wanted my real
home to be when I was growing up." She
smiled again. "Or at least that's probably what
a psychiatrist would say."

"And what would you say?"

"I'd say I enjoy doing things around my
home, personalizing it. It relaxes me to make
new curtains or refinish a piece of furniture or
cook a big pot of soup. Other than the occasional long weekend trip I usually stay home
on my vacation and work here. I might plant a
garden or paint a room." She shrugged. "It's
the way I play. How do you play?"

He looked at her blankly. "I don't know
that I do."

"You must. Everyone has to play now and
again."

Considering her question, he blew out a
long breath of air. "Well, okay, I usually go to
all the at-home basketball and football games.
That's fun for me."

Her brows arched and her eyes twinkled.
"Fun? Yelling for one team to kill the other?"

"Well, not *kill* the other team exactly, just
beat them six ways from Sunday. It's the skill
of the players and how they perform together
that excite me. Don't you like sports?"

"Sure. It's the way all those tight butts
look in those tight football uniforms that ex-

cite me. And of course let's not forget the great legs of the basketball players."

He came off the stool and looped his long arm around her neck in a mock stranglehold. "You couldn't resist, could you? You just had to say that."

She shrieked with laughter. "It happens to be true, and I didn't even get to the baseball players. The way they're always scratching and adjusting themselves is truly inspirational."

With a chuckle he released her. "Boy, remind me never to take you to a sporting event."

"Oh, come on. You can talk to me all you want to about the thrill of competition in sports, but you can't tell me that between plays you don't ogle the cheerleaders in their teeny little spandex uniforms."

He lifted his chin. "I plead the Fifth."

"Uh-huh."

"Is that soup nearly ready?"

She looked at him and shook her head. "*Men.*"

He put his finger up to his ear and rubbed as if trying to clear a blockage there. "Did I hear correctly? Was there a hint of disparagement in your tone?"

"There was a truckload of disparagement in my tone. The problem is you men think you should have exclusive rights in the ogling department."

"Actually I never knew there was such a thing as an *ogling department* before, but now that you mention it, exclusive rights do seem like a good idea."

"Dream on."

He laughed. "Maybe we should change the subject."

"Sure," she said airily. "I think I've made my point."

"Oh, there was a point?"

"Matthew," she said with angelic politeness, "would you like a bowl of soup?"

"Thank you, Samantha," he said, equally polite. "I would love a bowl. In fact, why don't we have it in front of a fire in the living room? While you're dishing it up, I'll go rub a few sticks together."

"Great idea. And if the caveman thing doesn't work, try the matches I have in the brass container to the right of the fireplace."

"Killjoy."

With a laugh she turned back to the stove. After the troublesome start they had had at the wedding, she would never have thought the weekend would turn out so perfectly. And the perfection went far beyond their lovemaking. She enjoyed everything about being with him. She enjoyed his teasing and the fact that she felt so completely free to tease him in return. And she enjoyed his quick mind, even when he was disagreeing with her.

Granted they had had no serious disagreements this weekend, but even with the specter of Richard between them like an eight-hundred-pound gorilla they had been able to put their differences aside and get along. It had been nice. More than nice actually.

Humming softly, she loaded a tray with two bowls of soup, bread, fruit, and cheese and took it into the living room. She found Matthew sitting on the floor with his back propped against the sofa, his gaze fixed on a cheerfully blazing fire in the stone-and-brick fireplace.

She handed him the tray and sat down beside him. "If you're getting anywhere near the withdrawal stage for the outside world, let me know. We could go for a walk or even take in a movie after we eat."

"I'm fine. The only thing I'm remotely missing is my Sunday comics, but—"

"Sunday comics!" She looked at him in amazement. "You too? I *love* the Sunday comics."

Speculation came into his eyes. "Maybe we should discuss this. Do you think the comics would qualify as an exemption from the 'shut the rest of the world out' rule?"

She settled back against the couch, bringing her bowl of soup with her. "It depends on what comic strips you read. If we read the same ones, I think we could make an exception. Also since there are two of us and only one set of comics, we might want to think about taking turns reading aloud to the other."

"Reading the comics aloud? No one has read the comics to me since I was a little boy."

She laughed. "And you think you're too grown up for that now?"

"No way will I ever be too grown up for that. I love the idea."

"Good. Let's eat, and then you can go out and search for the paper."

"Search?"

"My paper boy usually throws it in the general vicinity of my yard, but everyday it's an adventure to find it. One time I actually found it in the mailbox. Figure that one out."

"No problem. Adventures like that I can handle."

About an hour later Samantha stood at the kitchen window, gazing out at the gathering darkness. She had just finished rinsing their dishes and stacking them in the dishwasher, and Matthew was out searching for the paper.

He hadn't mentioned anything about going home yet, and she wondered if he would spend the night. Even though she had to get up early in the morning for the office, she hoped he would stay, because she was very sure that when he finally did leave, her home was going to seem quite empty.

Their meal had taken awhile because they had started talking about some of their all-time favorite comic strips. They had both been surprised and delighted to find out that they shared many favorites. Actually the whole weekend had been a surprise and delight to her. She didn't want it to end, but she knew that no matter what she might wish to the contrary, the clock would go on ticking and the earth would keep on turning and soon it would be time for both of them to go back to their real lives. She was dreading it.

She heard the front door close and hurried into the living room to meet him. "Did you have any trouble finding it?"

"No."

His furious expression brought her to an abrupt halt. "What's wrong?"

Without a word he peeled off the front section of the paper and handed it to her. She took it and looked down at the front page.

JUDGE RICHARD BARNETT DISAPPEARS.

TEN

Samantha's hand flew to her heart. "Oh, my God, *Richard*!" She quickly scanned the article. "This says Saturday afternoon he told his wife he was going out for a loaf of bread and a gallon of milk and hasn't been seen since. That means he's been missing over twenty-four hours."

"Where is he?"

"The police are investigating," she said, continuing to read, trying to pick up as many facts as quickly as possible.

"Where *is* he, Samantha?"

"What?" Uncomprehendingly she glanced up at Matthew, and slowly his accusation registered. "How would I know?"

"You were with him Saturday morning. He disappeared Saturday afternoon. Other than his wife you're probably one of the last persons to see him, and you two were awfully cozy in the park."

"What are you saying?" she asked, bewildered. "You think I *know* something about Richard's disappearance?"

"It makes sense to me."

Feeling a hollow disappointment, she stared at him. It seemed the weekend was going to end sooner than she had expected. "Of course it does. Let me just get my keys and I'll take you right to the place where I buried his body."

"Dammit, Samantha, I'm not saying you killed him."

"No? Are you sure? Or have you suddenly remembered that you and I were together Saturday afternoon and since then we've barely been out of each other's sight? Otherwise I'm sure I would have been at the top of your suspect list. But then, now that I think about it, I've been there for one reason or another ever since we met."

"Cut out the melodramatics, Samantha. Right from the beginning you've been stonewalling me on Barnett."

"Oh, good heavens, how *stupid* of me! Has there been a law passed I'm not aware of that says I must tell you everything you want to know?"

"All I'm saying is that you know more than you've told me."

She threw down the newspaper. "Well, no kidding, Dick Tracy. And exactly *why* should I tell you anything about a man who's a long-time friend of mine and whom you'd like nothing better than to crucify in your damned paper."

"I only want to get the truth out."

"You wouldn't know the truth if it was standing right in front of you."

She was standing right in front of him, he reflected, drawing a deep, steady breath, and she was furious with him. In addition she was obviously very worried about her friend, and here he was throwing one accusation after another at her. He held up a placating hand. "Okay, stop. Calm down."

"Calm *down*? No, I don't think so. We've just spent the last twenty-six hours or so having a great time, but the minute the real world intrudes and you get that damned story in your head again, you're off and running, accusing me right and left, turning into Matthew Stone, Intrepid Investigative Reporter, who stops at nothing to get his story." She threw a wild glance around the living room. "Where are *your* keys? Find them, along with your clothes, because I've just decided you're leaving."

He slipped his hands into his trouser pockets and eyed her levelly. "That's some temper you have there—very impressive—but I'm not leaving. At least not until we sort this out."

"Sort this out? What you really mean is until I tell you what you want to know. Sorry, Matthew, but I'm not going to do that. You can make me forget just about everything in bed, but that's definitely not going to happen again and unless you've got some sodium Pentothal up your sleeve—"

"Okay, okay." He touched her arm, but she shrugged away. He pointed toward the sofa. "Can we please sit down and talk for a minute? I'm sorry for jumping to conclusions."

"Jumping? No, no, no, Matthew. You made a bounding leap that took you so high, I'm surprised you didn't bump into a satellite or two."

He couldn't help but grin. "I was wrong, okay? I was wrong. And you, Samantha, are one tough lady."

"Tough? Because I won't tell you what you want to know? I suppose all the other women in your life have taken one look at those blue eyes of yours and have done anything you want." The moment the words were out of her mouth, she thought of his wife and regretted what she had said.

"No," he said with a surprising amount of gentleness and patience in his voice. "You're one tough lady because you know how to bring me down and put me in my place."

Forcefully reining in her temper, she crossed her arms beneath her breasts. "Something that obviously hasn't been done enough in your lifetime," she said without heat.

"I'm not going to argue with you. In fact I may never argue with you again. Now, can we please sit down?"

She eyed him warily. "Why?"

"I want to talk to you. You don't have to say anything in return, but I'd like it if you would listen. If your friend Richard is in danger, I may have a way to help him."

His statement got her immediate attention. A life in the balance was far more important than any disagreement. *"How?"*

He walked to the couch, sat down, and waited until she was settled beside him. "If Richard is still alive, and by that I mean if he hasn't committed suicide—"

"Richard wouldn't do that," she stated flatly. "He loves his family too much."

"I know that's what you want to believe, but remember, he was facing, at the very least, public humiliation and, at worst, criminal proceedings."

"Not criminal proceedings," she said emphatically. "He hadn't done anything legally wrong."

"He hadn't yet. But he was being blackmailed, and if events had proceeded and he had given in—"

"He never would have."

"Okay, I'll take your word for it."

She put her hand over his, wanting to make him understand. "Matthew, when I met Richard in the park Saturday morning, he told me he needed the weekend to tell his family everything and prepare them for the coming fallout. Because Monday morning he planned to go public with the blackmail attempt. After that he plans to retire."

"And that's why you wouldn't tell me anything? Because you didn't trust me to hold on to the information until he made it public?"

"Would you have?"

"Yes, if I had truly believed that he would indeed go public on Monday. That would accomplish what I had been trying to do in the first place, which was to get the truth out and prevent a travesty of justice. Believe it or not, Samantha, I don't get some vicarious thrill out of hurting people. And I'm very much aware that an investigation can cut across a lot of lives and lay open all sorts of wounds. It can open closet doors and let out skeletons. I try very hard to be as responsible as I know how. Sometimes, I hope, most of the time, if I've done my work and I'm really lucky, the pain of the exposure is deserved pain."

"But innocent people can have their lives ruined, and Richard's family is innocent."

"I don't mean to be cynical, but don't you think he should have thought of them before he got himself into this fix?"

"Yes, I do, and so does he. And as I've told you before, you *are* cynical, Matthew." Her expression was troubled. "I'm not sure you know how to trust anyone."

"That's not true."

"I think it is, but please, can we get back to how you can help Richard?"

"Right. Okay, if you're convinced that he hasn't committed suicide—"

"I am."

"Then that means the criminal cartel smelled a rat and snatched him before he could go public."

She eyed him solemnly. "That's what I was afraid of."

"Now, I know the police are on the job, but if they want to, the cartel can make people disappear forever and the police will never find them. But . . ." He trailed off as he followed a train of thought.

"But what?"

"I've got something the police don't have."

"What?"

"An informant inside the cartel. His name

is Joe Gates and he's got a vested interest in seeing Tate go down."

"That's great," she said, excited. "Contact him. Call him *now*. Find out where Richard is."

"It doesn't work like that. He contacts me. Any other way and he could be put in danger. And guess what? My beeper has been off."

She went pale as the full implication of what he was saying sank in. "Oh, no," she said softly. "You mean he could have been trying to get you all this time?"

"Don't worry. I plan to turn it back on right away, but first there's something I want you to realize. If the cartel snatched Barnett, as I think they have, because they felt like their blackmail wasn't going to work, they have no reason to keep him alive. He may already be on the bottom of one of our many lovely lakes around here."

Her skin lost even more color, until it was ashen. "No, that can't be."

He gave a mild curse directed solely at himself, then squeezed her hand reassuringly. "I'm sorry, honey. I should have had more tact. It's just something I think you have to prepare yourself for. The cartel doesn't play games. If the deal with Barnett wasn't going to work, they wouldn't want to waste any more time on him. They would want to get rid of him as soon as possible and try to set some other plan into action."

She slowly shook her head back and forth, rejecting completely what he was saying. "No, no. Not Richard. He's got to be okay."

"Unless . . . no, he wouldn't have any leverage with them unless he could convince them that he would go along with their plan after all and throw the trial. And once they're suspicious of him, that would be damned near impossible. Those people don't give second chances." He rubbed his forehead as he tried to consider all angles of the situation. "The paper said the police are protecting his family. That means the cartel couldn't threaten his family to get him to do what they want. And they must have figured out he confessed to his wife about the affair. . . ."

Her eyes widened. "What did you just say?"

"That they figured out—"

"No, no, *leverage*!" Her voice rose in excitement. "Matthew, Richard has *leverage*!"

"What?"

She jumped up. "I'll be right back. I've got to get my purse."

"Your purse?" Matthew watched curiously as she disappeared out of the room, then took the opportunity to locate his beeper and switch it on. He was back in the living room by the time she returned.

"Here it is," she said, holding up a small manila envelope. "He gave this to me in the park yesterday to hold for him."

"He gave it to you? But I didn't see him give you anything. Oh, wait a minute. . . ." His voice trailed off as he remembered that he had looked away several times, unable to watch her holding Barnett's hand and talking so intimately with him. "What is it?"

"All I know is that it's a microcassette audiotape. I can feel its shape through the envelope. He told me to hold it for him, and nothing else. Quite frankly with everything that's happened between you and me since, I forgot about it. I had no idea he was in any danger. He told me just to hold it for him."

He eyed her speculatively. "Do you have something that will play it?"

"You want to listen to it?"

He nodded. "I'd like to get an idea exactly how much leverage Barnett has so that we can make an educated guess about his present position. I've turned on my beeper. With any luck Gates will call me soon, but even if he does, there's no guarantee he knows anything that will help us."

She looked at the envelope in her hand, then back at him. "Under no circumstances can this tape be made public, Matthew. At least not until Richard is safe."

"Don't you think I know that? The real question is are you going to trust me?"

She hesitated only briefly before she handed him the envelope. "I'll get my microcassette player."

Stunned, he watched her leave the room. In a very short time they had experienced a range of emotions that might have left another couple in pieces. And now they were dealing with a matter of life and death. He couldn't think of one reason why she should trust him with the life of her friend, but miracle of miracles, she did, and he was sobered by the thought. There was no way he would betray her trust.

She returned, and minutes later they had finished listening to the tape.

"Okay, so now we know Richard is safe," Samantha said. "The tape virtually guarantees it. He must have set up a meeting somewhere they considered safe and then used a concealed voice-activated tape recorder without their knowledge."

Matthew shook his head in wonder. "My hat is off to him for even attempting such a thing, much less pulling it off. A judge would have to rule this tape as evidence, but at the very least it can incriminate a lot of people. The man Barnett was talking to is clearly identified."

"Richard is a good man who made a mistake, and now he's trying to do the most honorable thing. I tried to tell you."

With a smile he gently caressed her cheek. "Do all your friends get such unstinting loyalty from you? Never mind. I know the answer, it's yes." His smile faded and his hand dropped away. "Unfortunately there's a problem. With this tape Barnett and the cartel have a stalemate."

"I don't understand. I thought the tape would be Richard's insurance."

"Oh, he had the right idea by making the tape. It has probably bought him time by making them carefully weigh their options. They can't let him go. They have their own twisted idea of credibility, and it's everything to them. No one, no matter what the circumstances, can double-cross them without paying."

"But they can't kill him! They've got to know that the day his body is found, the tape will be made public."

"Yeah. But what if they kill him and the body is never found? They can do that; they've done it before. In effect they would bury the body and cut their losses, and the person who has the tape wouldn't know for sure if Barnett is alive or dead. That person—you—wouldn't want to risk Barnett's life, so you'd sit on the tape, at least for a while. That would give them time to reorganize so completely, it would take years to penetrate their organization as far as the law has gotten this time. They'd write Tate off, and in the end they'd win. Of course Barnett would be dead, but they'd win, and sooner or later I'm betting that's just what they'll opt for."

A sob escaped from her throat. *"No."*

He reached for her hand. "Keep the faith, honey. If Gates will call, we may still have a chance—"

His beeper went off, and they both jumped. Quickly recovering, he grabbed for it and looked at the number. "Damn, it's the paper. I'm sure they're wondering what's happened to me. They know I've been on this story."

"Will you call them?"

"In a minute. Listen, Samantha, there's something I want to say to you. I want to thank you for trusting me enough to let me hear the tape."

She had made the decision in an instant, but even so she had known it was important. He had told her that he thought love was supposed to be about sharing and trusting and helping each other, and she completely agreed. Love. . . . "At the start of the weekend I might have made a different decision."

He chuckled softly. "No, there's no *might* about it. You *would* have made a different decision."

"I think we can both agree that this hasn't

been an ordinary weekend," she said carefully. "I know you better now. Timewise it hasn't even been a *full* weekend, but—"

The beeper went off again. He grabbed it and studied the number. "I don't recognize the number, but it's got to be him." He glanced at her. "What were you going to say?"

There were a lot of things she needed to say, emotions she needed to decipher. But then again did she really need to do that? There was one powerful truth that shone through all her confusion. She loved him. She loved him with all her heart.

"We'll get back to the discussion later," she said. "Right now you need a phone. Use the one in the kitchen," she said, rising at the same time he did and leading the way. In the kitchen she thrust the receiver at him, then as he punched out the number, she nervously twined her fingers together.

Matthew's face lit up as he heard Gates's voice on the other end of the line, and he nodded at Samantha. "Great, it is you! What have you got? Do you know where they're holding Barnett? Is he alive?"

Samantha saw his hands tighten on the receiver, and then he nodded to her again. Gates *did* know, she thought thankfully.

"Yeah, I'm sorry I've been out of touch,

but listen, can you help? Tell me what you know."

He fell silent again, listening, and Samantha said a short prayer that they'd be able to get to Richard in time. He was a good man, and his family would stand behind him.

"Okay," he said at last. "I'll see what I can do." He paused. "No, no, don't worry. No matter what happens, I won't implicate you."

He hung up the phone and turned to look at Samantha. "I have some good news and I have some not-so-good news."

"Tell me."

"Gates told me where they took Barnett. It's a warehouse down in the industrial district. I know where it is. The not-so-good news is that he's not sure if Barnett is still alive."

She barely managed to control the shiver of fear that rushed through her. "We've got to help him."

Her skin was very pale, but determination was written in every line of her body. And he loved her very much. He badly wanted to take her in his arms and tell her, but she wasn't going to be able to concentrate on anything until she knew her friend was safe. He turned back to the phone and punched in another number. "We're going to need some help, but I don't want the whole Dallas Police Department in on this." He began to talk as soon as his call was answered.

Samantha listened without asking any questions. Every minute that passed lessened Richard's chance of staying alive. She couldn't regret the time she and Matthew had spent with their beepers turned off and the world shut out, though it had prevented them from knowing about Richard earlier. All she could do now was believe that all would end well. And she had to be satisfied with the fact that Matthew was doing everything in his power to help Richard. It would be enough, she prayed. It had to be.

Matthew hung up and turned back to her. "Okay, here's the deal. I've got a cop friend who owes me a couple of big favors, and it's a damned good thing, too, because I've asked him to go out on a real fragile limb for me. I've given him the whole setup, but I've asked them to pass the information to only a select number of people he trusts to do things right. A dog-and-pony show complete with a SWAT team will ruin this deal."

"So what's going to happen?"

"I told him I'd like to be there. I'm going to get dressed and meet him a block or two away from the warehouse." He headed toward the bedroom. "I'll call you when it's all over and let you know what happened."

"I'm coming with you," she said, following him.

"No, Samantha, you're not. It's too dangerous."

She disappeared into her closet and came back out with a pair of tennis shoes and a smile on her face. "I'll make you a deal. I won't go anywhere you don't."

Matthew was still trying to change her mind when they drove up behind his friend's unmarked police car.

"Stay put," he ordered, and kissed her.

"If you're going in, so am I."

He put his hand up to her face. "Listen to me, Samantha. My friend won't let you go in, but he'll let me as long as I stay back. He trusts me not to do anything stupid."

"But you could be hurt."

"No. I've done things like this before. I know to stay back and be careful."

She wrapped her fingers around his wrist and held on to him. "Promise me you won't get hurt."

He nodded and kissed her again. "I promise."

He conferred with his friend, then a group of policemen advanced on the warehouse with him not too far behind.

Samantha wasn't even aware of breathing,

but she *was* aware of everything else. She jumped at the slightest sound. Around her, colors brightened, then faded to sepia, then brightened again. If she moved at all, her movements were slow and heavy. It was bad enough to think that Richard might be hurt or, worse, dead. But if anything were to happen to Matthew, she wouldn't be able to bear it. Seconds ticked by, becoming minutes. And then at last she saw Richard emerge from the warehouse, pale, haggard, exhausted, but nevertheless alive, with Matthew right behind him. With an exclamation of happiness she bolted from the car and ran to Richard.

And watching, Matthew could only smile.

It was nearly midnight by the time Samantha arrived back at her house. She felt emotionally drained as if she had no more adrenaline left in her body. Matthew was with her. Soon no doubt he would leave for the paper so that he could write his story, but for her own peace of mind there were things she wanted resolved.

In the living room she turned to face him. "I can't thank you enough for helping Richard."

He sank onto the couch and wearily ran his fingers through his hair. "I was glad to be able to do it. Thank God we found him alive."

She nodded. "I know you're probably eager to get your story written—"

"What story?"

She looked at him in surprise. "The story about Richard and the blackmail attempt."

He patted the couch beside him. "Come sit down."

They had shared many things this past weekend. Amazingly she could hardly remember when he hadn't been a part of her life. And even though she had no idea what he wanted, it was the most natural thing in the world for her to join him on the couch.

"The police were involved tonight in rescuing Barnett," he said. "That means to a certain extent their activities were monitored. By the time we got out of the warehouse, I saw reporters from at least two local television stations there. Barnett's rescue will lead off the morning news. The public will know all about it by the time they go to work tomorrow. If I were to write an article on it, all I would be doing would be rehashing what is already known, and that's not my style. No, I'll let someone else do it."

"But the television reporters don't know about the blackmail attempt. You do."

"Yes." He stroked his hand over her hair in a gentle caress. "By the way, why haven't you asked me not to report the blackmail attempt or the reason behind it?"

She paused to choose her words carefully. "I understand how important your job is to you. I trusted you with Richard's life when I let you listen to that tape, and you helped him. After that I have no right to ask you not to do your job."

"I appreciate that more than you can know, but the truth is I had already decided not to write the story. The only reason I would have exposed the blackmail and the affair behind it would have been to stop a miscarriage of justice. But now that Barnett is going to retire, he won't be sitting on Tate's trial. In this case telling the public the truth behind the blackmail wouldn't do any good, and it would only serve to hurt his family without purpose."

"That's very kind of you."

He smiled at the hint of surprise in her voice. "I told you that I try to be responsible."

"I'm impressed."

His smile broadened. "Then I'm happy." But he was also impatient and more than a little anxious, he reflected, and he was almost physically incapable of waiting to tell her what was uppermost in his mind. "There's something else, Samantha."

A cold dread gripped her heart. "Matthew, you don't owe me any explanations. I knew this weekend would end sooner or later and that you'd leave."

He put his fingers to her lips, quieting her. "I need to get this out, so, please, just listen. More than anything else in the world right now I need to tell you that I love you."

"You . . . ?" His words had shocked her.

He eyed her worriedly. "I'm sorry if the idea upsets you, but this is something outside my control. I love you with all my heart. I don't know—maybe I should have waited a little while longer to tell you. Things between us have gone very fast. Maybe I should have waited until we weren't so tired or arranged a romantic dinner or something. But the truth is I simply couldn't wait, because if you're going to try to kick me out again, I want to start trying to change your mind immediately."

Overwhelmed with relief and happiness, she burst out laughing. "I'm not even a *little* bit upset."

"No?"

"No." Lovingly she lifted her hand to his face. "I knew what a good marriage—a good match—should be because I grew up with a mother and father who didn't have one. I believed I would know the man for me when I met him. But with you my instincts fell apart. It's why I fought so hard against you and tried to fix you up with my friends. I accused you of not seeing the truth when it was standing in front of you, but, Matthew, I couldn't see the truth either."

"And what is the truth?" he asked, still uncertain about her reaction.

"I love you," she said simply. "I don't know how or when it happened, but I love you."

He let out a long sigh of relief. "Maybe it happened to you the same time it happened to me—that first day outside the courthouse. I looked up and saw you walking toward me out of the sun and I should have known right then and there that something extraordinary was about to happen. You challenged me and you enchanted me, and I was a goner."

"I think you're right about it happening that first day. You were being completely annoying, but you definitely captured my attention and you've had it ever since."

"I know I'm doing this all wrong," he said huskily, drawing her to him. "I don't even have a ring to give you, but I've got to know—how do you feel about spending the rest of your life with me?"

She laughed, and slid her arms around his neck. "I feel great about it, stupendous in fact."

And in the end, she thought, after all the arguing and the lovemaking and conflicts, it was as simple and as uncomplicated as that.

EPILOGUE

Six months later.
Samantha came toward him out of the sun, and this time he didn't shield his eyes. He could see her quite plainly, and what he saw was the woman he loved more than life itself.

They had met and fallen in love one enchanted autumn, and now it was spring and they were getting married in her gardens. Hedges of lilac were in bloom, and white jasmine climbed nearby trellises. Herbs and still more flowers saturated the air with fragrance.

Samantha was wearing a long ivory dress of antique lace and chiffon sewn with iridescent pearls and sequins that gleamed and glittered in the sun. Gold-and-cream lilies and daisies were twined in her hair, and her bouquet was made of daisies, baby's breath, and lilies. Everywhere gold, ivory, and peach-colored ribbons were tied in bows, and their ends fluttered in the breeze.

A string quartet played softly, romantically. And as Leona and Alfred looked on along with other members of their family and friends, they exchanged vows that would bind them together for the rest of their lives.

Matthew smiled down at Samantha, knowing that for now and forever each season of their life would bring new and wondrous enchantment. He could hardly wait.

THE EDITOR'S CORNER

It's a magical time of year, with ghosts and goblins, haunted houses and trick-or-treating. What better way to indulge yourself than with our four enchanting romances coming next month! These sexy, mystical men offer our heroines their own unique blend of passion and love. Truly, you are going to be LOVESWEPT by these stories that are guaranteed to heat your blood and keep you warm through the chilly days ahead.

The wonderfully unique Ruth Owen starts off our lineup with **SORCERER,** LOVESWEPT #714. Jillian Polanski has always been able to hold her own with Ian Sinclair, but when they enter the machine he's created to explore an unreal world, she becomes his damsel in distress and he the knight who'll risk his life to save hers. In this magic realm Ian's embrace stirs buried longings and dangerous desires, but now she must trust this dark lord with her dreams. Once again Ruth will draw you into a breathtaking adventure that is both playful and heartbreaking.

Marcia Evanick's hero walks right **OUT OF A DREAM,** LOVESWEPT #715! With a mysterious crash Clayton Williams appears in Alice Jorgensen's parlor on Halloween night—and convinces the lady in the rabbit suit that he'll be nothing but trouble. Unwilling to let her escape his passionate pursuit, Clayton insists on moving into her boardinghouse and vows to learn her secrets. Can she risk loving a daredevil with stars in his eyes? Marcia weaves bewitching magic and celebrates the delightful mystery of true love.

Jan Hudson is on a **HOT STREAK,** LOVESWEPT #716, with a hero who sizzles. Amy Jordan wonders how an out-of-this-world gorgeous man could look so heartbroken, then races out into the rain to rescue him! After disaster struck his research, Dr. Neil Larkin felt shattered . . . but once Amy ignites a flame of hope with kisses that would melt holes in a lab beaker, he is enchanted—struck by the lightning of steamy, sultry attraction no science could explain. Jan does it again with this touching and funny story that makes for irresistible reading.

Last but never least is **IMAGINARY LOVER,** LOVESWEPT #717, by the ever popular Sandra Chastain. Dusty O'Brian can't believe her aunt has left the old house to her and to Dr. Nick Elliott! The pain burning in the doctor's mesmerizing dark eyes echoes her own grief, but she's been pushing people away for too long to reach out to him—and he needs her too fiercely to confess his hunger. Is she his forbidden desire sent by fate, or the only woman who can make him whole? Sandra evokes this romantic fantasy with stunning power and unforgettable passion.

Happy reading!

With warmest wishes,

Beth de Guzman

Senior Editor

P.S. Don't miss the women's novels coming your way in November: **PURE SIN,** from the award-winning Susan Johnson, is a sensuous tale of thrilling seduction set in nineteenth-century Montana; **SCANDAL IN SILVER,** from bestselling author Sandra Chastain, is her second Once Upon a Time Romance and takes its cue from *Seven Brides for Seven Brothers;* **THE WINDFLOWER** is a beautifully written romance from the bestselling Sharon and Tom Curtis in which two worlds collide when an innocent lady is kidnapped by the pirate she has sworn to bring to justice. We'll be giving you a sneak peek at these wonderful books in next month's LOVESWEPTs. And immediately following this page, look for a preview of the terrific romances from Bantam that are *available now!*

Don't miss these spectacular books
by your favorite Bantam authors

On sale in September:
THIEF OF HEARTS
by *Teresa Medeiros*

COURTING MISS HATTIE
by *Pamela Morsi*

VIRGIN BRIDE
by *Tamara Leigh*

TERESA MEDEIROS

THIEF OF HEARTS

"Ms. Medeiros casts a spell with her poignant
writing."—*Rendezvous*

*From the storm-lashed decks of a pirate schooner to the
elegant grounds of an English estate comes a spellbinding
tale of love and deception . . . as only the remarkable
bestselling author Teresa Medeiros can tell it. . . .*

"I've heard enough about your cowardly tactics, Captain Doom, to know that your favored opponents are helpless women and innocent children afraid of ghosts."

A loose plank creaked behind her, startling her. If he had touched her then, she feared she would have burst into tears.

But it was only the mocking whisper of his breath that stirred her hair. "And which are you, Miss Snow? Innocent? Helpless? Or both?" When his provocative question met with stony silence, he resumed his pacing. " 'Tis customary to scream and weep when one is abducted by brigands, yet you've done neither. Why is that?"

Lucy didn't care to admit that she was afraid he'd embroider a skull and crossbones on her lips. "If I might have gained anything by screaming, you'd have left me gagged, wouldn't you? It's obvious by the motion of the deck that the ship is at full sail, precluding immediate rescue. And I've never found tears to be of any practical use."

"How rare." The note in his voice might have been one of mockery or genuine admiration. "Logic and intelligence wrapped up in such a pretty package. Tell me, is your father in the habit of allowing you to journey alone on a navy frigate? Young ladies of quality do not travel such a distance unchaperoned. Does he care so little for your reputation?

Lucy almost blurted out that her father cared for nothing *but* her reputation, but to reveal such a painful truth to this probing stranger would have been like laying an old wound bare.

"The captain's mother was traveling with us." Fat lot of good that had done her, Lucy thought. The senile old woman had probably slept through the attack. "The captain of the *Tiberius* is a dear friend of my father's. He's known me since I was a child. I can promise you that should any of the men under his command so much as smile at me in what might be deemed an improper manner, he'd have them flogged."

"Purely for your entertainment, I'm sure."

Lucy winced at the unfair cut. "I fear my tastes in amusement don't run to torture, as yours are rumored to," she replied sweetly.

"Touché, Miss Snow. Perhaps you're not so helpless after all. If we could only ascertain your innocence with such flair . . ."

He let the unspoken threat dangle, and Lucy swallowed a retort. She couldn't seem to stop her tart tongue from running rampant. She'd do well to remember that this man held both her life and her virtue captive in his fickle hands.

His brisk footsteps circled her, weaving a dizzying

spell as she struggled to follow his voice. "Perhaps you'd care to explain why your noble papa deprived himself of your charming wit for the duration of your voyage."

"Father took ill before we could leave Cornwall. A stomach grippe. He saw no logic in my forfeiting my passage, but feared travel by sea would only worsen his condition."

"How perceptive of him. It might even have proved fatal." He circled her again. His footsteps ceased just behind her. Doom's clipped tones softened. "So he sent you in his stead. Poor, sweet Lucy."

Lucy wasn't sure what jarred her most—the rueful note of empathy in his voice or hearing her Christian name caressed by his devilish tongue. "If you're going to murder me, do get on with it," she snapped. "You can eulogize me *after* I'm gone."

The chair vibrated as he closed his hands over its back. Lucy started as if he'd curled them around her bare throat. "Is that what they say about me, Miss Snow? That I'm a murderer?"

She pressed her eyes shut beneath the blindfold, beset by a curious mix of dread and anticipation. "Among other things."

"Such as?"

"A ghost," she whispered.

He leaned over her shoulder from behind and pressed his cheek to hers. The prickly softness of his beard chafed her tender skin. His masculine scent permeated her senses. "What say you, Lucy Snow? Am I spirit or man?"

There was nothing spectral about his touch. Its blatant virility set Lucy's raw nerves humming. She'd never been touched with such matter-of-fact intimacy by anyone.

The odd little catch in her breath ruined her prim reply. "I sense very little of the spiritual about you, sir."

"And much of the carnal, no doubt."

His hand threaded through the fragile shield of her hair to find her neck. His warm fingers gently rubbed her nape as if to soothe away all of her fears and melt her defenses, leaving her totally vulnerable to him. Lucy shuddered, shaken by his tenderness, intrigued by his boldness, intoxicated by his brandy-heated breath against her ear.

"Tell me more of the nefarious doings of Captain Doom," he coaxed.

She drew in a shaky breath, fighting for any semblance of the steely poise she had always prided herself on. "They say you can skewer your enemies with a single glance."

"Quite flattering, but I fear I have to use more conventional means." His probing fingertips cut a tingling swath through the sensitive skin behind her ears. "Do go on."

Lucy's honesty betrayed her. "They say you've been known to ravish ten virgins in one night." As soon as the words were out, she cringed, wondering what had possessed her to confess such a shocking thing.

Instead of laughing, as she expected, he framed her delicate jaw in his splayed fingers and tilted her head back.

His voice was both tender and solemn, mocking them both. "Ah, but then one scrawny virgin such as yourself would only whet my appetite."

"They also swear you won't abide babbling," Lucy blurted out, knowing she was doing just that.

"That you'll sew up the lips of anyone who dares to defy you."

His breath grazed her lips. "What a waste that would be in your case. Especially when I can think of far more pleasurable ways to silence them."

COURTING MISS HATTIE
BY
PAMELA MORSI

The nationally bestselling author of WILD OATS

"A refreshing new voice in romance."
—Jude Deveraux

*Award-winning author Pamela Morsi has won readers'
hearts with her unforgettable novels—filled with romance,
humor, and her trademark down-to-earth charm. And
with her classic COURTING MISS HATTIE, Morsi
pairs an unlikely bride and an irresistible suitor who learn
that love can be found in the most unexpected places.*

"All right, explain to me about kissing."

"There are three kinds of kisses."

"Right," she said skeptically. "Don't tell me,
they're called hook, line, and sinker."

"That's fishing. This is kissing. I know a lot about
both, and if you want to know what I know, listen up
and mind your manners."

He'd released her hands, and she folded them
primly in her lap, sitting up straight like a good pupil.
Her expression was still patently skeptical, though.
"Okay, three kinds of kisses," she repeated, as if trying to remember.

"There's the peck, the peach, and the malvalva."

Hattie didn't bother to control her giggle. "The
mal-whata?"

"Malvalva. But we haven't got to that one yet."

"And with luck, we never will. This is pure silliness," she declared.

"You admitted yourself that you know nothing about kissing," Reed said. "It's easy, but you've got to learn the basics."

"I'm all ears."

"Ears are good, but I think we ought to start with lips."

"Reed!"

There was laughter in his eyes as a flush colored her face, but he continued his discourse matter-of-factly, as if he were explaining a new farming method. "Okay, the peck is the most common kiss. It's the kind you're already familiar with. That's what you gave your folks and such. You just purse your lips together and make a little pop sound, like this." He demonstrated several times, his lips pursing together seductively, then releasing a little kiss to the air.

Hattie found the sight strangely titillating. "Okay, I see what you mean," she said.

"Show me," he instructed.

She made several kisses in the air while Reed inspected her style. "I feel like an idiot!" she exclaimed after a moment. "I must look so silly."

"Well," he admitted, "kissing the air is a little silly. But when it's against your sweetheart's lips, it doesn't feel silly at all."

She made several more self-conscious attempts as he watched her lips. "Is this the way?" she asked.

"I think you'll do fine with that." He shifted his position a bit and looked past her for a moment. "That's a good first kiss for someone like Drayton," he said seriously, then grinned. "Don't let him get the good stuff until later."

She opened her mouth to protest, but he cut her short. "Now, the second kind of kiss is called a peach. It's a bit different from the peck." He reached out and grasped her shoulders, scooting her a little closer. "This is the one that lovers use a lot."

"Why do they call it a peach?" she asked curiously.

His smile was warm and lazy. " 'Cause it's so sweet and juicy."

"Juicy?" she repeated worriedly.

"Just a little. First, open your mouth a little, about this wide." He demonstrated.

"Open my mouth?"

"Yes, just a little. So you can taste the other person."

"Taste?"

"Just a little. Try it."

She held her lips open as he'd shown her. He nodded encouragement. "That's about right," he said. "Now you need to suck a bit."

"Suck?"

"Just a bit."

She shook her head, waving away the whole suggestion. "This is ridiculous, Reed. I can't do it."

He slid closer to her. "It only feels ridiculous because you're doing it without a partner. Here . . ." He again grasped her shoulders and pulled her near. "Try it on me. You won't feel nearly as silly, and it'll give you some practice."

"You want me to kiss you?"

"Just for practice. Open your mouth again."

She did as she was told, her eyes wide in surprise. Reed lowered his head toward hers, his lips also parted invitingly. "When I get close like this," he said, his breath warm on her cheek, "you turn your head a little."

"Why?"

"So we won't bump noses."

Following his lead, she angled her head. "That's right. Perfect," he whispered the instant before his lips touched hers.

It was a gentle touch, and only a touch, before he moved back slightly. "Don't forget to suck," he murmured.

"Suck."

"Like a peach."

"Like a peach."

Then his mouth was on hers again. She felt the tenderness of his lips and the insistent pressure of the vacuum they created. She did as he'd instructed, her mouth gently pulling at his. A little angle, a little suction, a little juicy, and very, very warm.

"What do you think?" he whispered against her mouth.

"Nice" was all she got out before he continued his instruction.

They pulled apart finally, and Hattie opened her eyes in wonder. The blood was pounding in her veins. Staring at Reed, she saw mirrored on his face the same pleased confusion she felt. "I did it right?" she asked, but she knew the answer already. Kissing might be new to her, but it was impossible not to believe that what she felt was exactly why courting couples were always looking for a moment of privacy.

"Yes," Reed answered. He slid his arms around her back and pulled her more firmly against his chest. "Do you think you can do it again?"

VIRGIN BRIDE

BY

TAMARA LEIGH

"Fresh, exciting . . . wonderfully sensual . . . sure
to be noticed in the romance genre."
—Amanda Quick

Tamara Leigh burst onto the romance scene with WAR-
RIOR BRIDE and was praised by authors and critics alike.
Now with VIRGIN BRIDE she offers another electrifying
tale of a woman who would give anything to avoid being
sent to a convent—even her virtue.

"Enough!" The anguished cry wrenched itself from
Graeye's throat. All her life she had been looked upon
with suspicion, but now, with her world crashing
down around her, she simply could take no more ac-
cusations—and most especially from this man . . . a
man to whom she had given her most precious possession.

Driven by renewed anger, she was unable to check
the reckless impulse to wipe the derision from
Balmaine's face. She raised her arm and a moment
later was amazed at the ease with which she landed
her palm to his face. With the exception of William,
never before had she struck another.

"I am but a human being cursed to bear a mark set
upon my face—not by the devil but by God." In her
tirade she paid no heed to the spreading red left by

her hand, or the sparkle of fury that leaped to Balmaine's eyes.

" 'Tis a mark of birth, naught else," she continued. "You have nothing to fear from me that you would not fear from another."

"So the little one has claws, eh?" He made the observation between clenched teeth. " 'Tis as I thought."

One moment Graeye was upright, face-to-face with this hard, angry man, and the next she was on her back, that same face above hers as those spectacular orbs bored into her.

"Had I the time or inclination," he said, "I might be tempted to tame that terrible temper of yours. But as I've neither, you will have to content yourself with this."

Temper? But she didn't—Graeye had no time to ponder his estimation of her nature before she felt his mouth on hers. The thought to resist never entered her mind.

When he urged her to open to him, she parted her lips with a sigh and took him inside. Slowly his tongue began an exploration of the sensitive places within—places he knew better than she.

Turning away from the insistent voices that urged her to exercise caution, she welcomed the invasion and recklessly wound her arms around him, pressing herself to his hard curves. When his hand slid between them to stroke that place below her belly, she arched against it.

Then, as abruptly as it had begun, it was over, and she was left to stare up at the man who had so effortlessly disengaged himself from her.

In the blink of an eye he had turned from passionate lover to cold and distant adversary. How was it he had such control over his emotions when she had none? Was she too long suppressed?

"I may have fallen prey to your wiles last eventide," he said, smoothing his hands down his tunic. "But I assure you I have no intention of paying the price you would ask for such an unfortunate tryst. Your scheme has failed, Lady Graeye."

To gather her wits about her after such a thorough attack upon her traitorous senses was not an easy thing, but the impact of his words made it less difficult than it would otherwise have been. Doing her utmost to put behind what had just occurred, she lifted herself from the bench and stood before him.

"You err," she said in a terribly small voice that made her wince. Drawing a deep breath, she delivered her next words with more assurance. "There is naught I want from you that you have not already given."

His eyes narrowed. "And what do you think you have stolen from me?"

She lifted her chin a notch, refusing to be drawn into a futile argument as to whether she had stolen or been given his caresses.

"Though you do not believe me," she said, "I tell you true that I did not know who you were until this morn. 'Twas freedom from the Church I hoped to gain, not a husband—that is what you gave me."

Nostrils flaring, Balmaine gave a short bark of laughter. "Be assured, Lady Graeye," he said as he adjusted his sword on its belt, "you will return to the abbey. Though you are no longer pure enough to become a nun, there will be a place for you there at the convent. You will go . . . even if I have to drag you there myself."

The convent . . . She took a step nearer him. "'Tis not your decision whether—"

His hand sliced impatiently through the air. "Ultimately *everything* that has anything to do with Medland is under my control. You had best accept it and resign yourself to entering the convent."

Her heart began to hammer against her ribs. Was what he said true? Could he, in fact, usurp her father's rights over her? If so, since he was determined to return her to Arlecy, all would have been for naught. Biting her lip, she bowed her head and focused upon the hilt of his sword.

"Then I would ask you to reconsider, Baron Balmaine, and allow me to remain with my father. He is not well and is in need of someone—"

"The decision has been made," he interrupted again, then turned on his heel and strode away.

Even if Graeye could have contained the anger flaring through her, she would not have. There was nothing left to lose. "You have a rather nasty penchant for rudely interrupting when one is trying to speak," she snapped. "'Tis something you really ought to work at correcting."

Seething, she stared at his back, willing him to turn again.

He did not disappoint her, returning to tower over her and looking every bit the barbarian. "In future, if you have anything to say to me, Lady Graeye, I would prefer you address my face rather than my back. Do you understand?"

Though she knew he could easily crush her between his hands if he so desired—and at that moment he certainly looked tempted to—Graeye managed to quell the instinct to cower. After all, considering the fate that awaited her, it hardly mattered what he might do. She gathered the last shreds of her courage about her and drew herself up, utilizing every hair's breadth of height she had.

"In future, you say?" She gave a short, bitter laugh. "As we have no future together, Baron, 'tis an entirely absurd request. Or should I say 'order'?"

His lids snapped down to narrow slits, a vein in his forehead leaping to life. "Sheathe your claws, little cat," he hissed, his clenched fists testament to the control he was exercising. "The day is still young and we have games yet to play."

Then he was walking away again, leaving her to stare after him with a face turned fearful.

And don't miss these sizzling
romances from Bantam Books,
on sale in October:

WANTED
by the nationally bestselling author

Patricia Potter

"One of the romance genre's finest talents."
—*Romantic Times*

SCANDAL IN SILVER
by the highly acclaimed

Sandra Chastain

"Sandra Chastain's characters' steamy relationships
are the stuff dreams are made of."
—*Romantic Times*

THE WINDFLOWER
by the award-winning

Sharon & Tom Curtis

"Sharon and Tom's talent is immense."
—LaVyrle Spencer

OFFICIAL RULES

To enter the sweepstakes below carefully follow all instructions found elsewhere in this offer.

The **Winners Classic** will award prizes with the following approximate maximum values: 1 Grand Prize: $26,500 (or $25,000 cash alternate); 1 First Prize: $3,000; 5 Second Prizes: $400 each; 35 Third Prizes: $100 each; 1,000 Fourth Prizes: $7.50 each. Total maximum retail value of Winners Classic Sweepstakes is $42,500. Some presentations of this sweepstakes may contain individual entry numbers corresponding to one or more of the aforementioned prize levels. To determine the Winners, individual entry numbers will first be compared with the winning numbers preselected by computer. For winning numbers not returned, prizes will be awarded in random drawings from among all eligible entries received. Prize choices may be offered at various levels. If a winner chooses an automobile prize, all license and registration fees, taxes, destination charges and, other expenses not offered herein are the responsibility of the winner. If a winner chooses a trip, travel must be complete within one year from the time the prize is awarded. Minors must be accompanied by an adult. Travel companion(s) must also sign release of liability. Trips are subject to space and departure availability. Certain black-out dates may apply.

The following applies to the sweepstakes named above:

No purchase necessary. You can also enter the sweepstakes by sending your name and address to: P.O. Box 508, Gibbstown, N.J. 08027. Mail each entry separately. Sweepstakes begins 6/1/93. Entries must be received by 12/30/94. Not responsible for lost, late, damaged, misdirected, illegible or postage due mail. Mechanically reproduced entries are not eligible. All entries become property of the sponsor and will not be returned.

Prize Selection/Validations: Selection of winners will be conducted no later than 5:00 PM on January 28, 1995, by an independent judging organization whose decisions are final. Random drawings will be held at 1211 Avenue of the Americas, New York, N.Y. 10036. Entrants need not be present to win. Odds of winning are determined by total number of entries received. Circulation of this sweepstakes is estimated not to exceed 200 million. All prizes are guaranteed to be awarded and delivered to winners. Winners will be notified by mail and may be required to complete an affidavit of eligibility and release of liability which must be returned within 14 days of date on notification or alternate winners will be selected in a random drawing. Any prize notification letter or any prize returned to a participating sponsor, Bantam Doubleday Dell Publishing Group, Inc., its participating divisions or subsidiaries, or the independent judging organization as undeliverable will be awarded to an alternate winner. Prizes are not transferable. No substitution for prizes except as offered or as may be necessary due to unavailability, in which case a prize of equal or greater value will be awarded. Prizes will be awarded approximately 90 days after the drawing. All taxes are the sole responsibility of the winners. Entry constitutes permission (except where prohibited by law) to use winners' names, hometowns, and likenesses for publicity purposes without further or other compensation. Prizes won by minors will be awarded in the name of parent or legal guardian.

Participation: Sweepstakes open to residents of the United States and Canada, except for the province of Quebec. Sweepstakes sponsored by Bantam Doubleday Dell Publishing Group, Inc., (BDD), 1540 Broadway, New York, NY 10036. Versions of this sweepstakes with different graphics and prize choices will be offered in conjunction with various solicitations or promotions by different subsidiaries and divisions of BDD. Where applicable, winners will have their choice of any prize offered at level won. Employees of BDD, its divisions, subsidiaries, advertising agencies, independent judging organization, and their immediate family members are not eligible.

Canadian residents, in order to win, must first correctly answer a time limited arithmetical skill testing question. Void in Puerto Rico, Quebec and wherever prohibited or restricted by law. Subject to all federal, state, local and provincial laws and regulations. For a list of major prize winners (available after 1/29/95): send a self-addressed, stamped envelope entirely separate from your entry to: Sweepstakes Winners, P.O. Box 517, Gibbstown, NJ 08027. Requests must be received by 12/30/94. DO NOT SEND ANY OTHER CORRESPONDENCE TO THIS P.O. BOX.

SWP 7/93

Don't miss these fabulous Bantam women's fiction titles

On Sale in September

THIEF OF HEARTS

by **Teresa Medeiros**, bestselling author of *A Whisper of Roses*

"Ms. Medeiros casts a spell with her poignant writing."
—Rendezvous

From the storm-lashed decks of a pirate schooner to the elegant grounds of an English estate comes a spellbinding tale of love and deception as only the remarkable Teresa Medeiros can tell it.

❏ *56332-7 $5.50/6.99 in Canada*

COURTING MISS HATTIE

by **Pamela Morsi**, bestselling author of *Wild Oats*

"A refreshing new voice in romance."—Jude Deveraux

Pamela Morsi has won readers' hearts with her unforgettable novels—filled with romance, humor, and her trademark down-to-earth charm. And with *Courting Miss Hattie*, Morsi pairs an improbable bride and an irresistible suitor who learn that love can be found in the most unlikely places.

❏ *29000-2 $5.50/6.99 in Canada*

VIRGIN BRIDE

by **Tamara Leigh**

"Fresh, exciting...wonderfully sensual...sure to be noticed in the romance genre."—Amanda Quick

Tamara Leigh burst onto the romance scene with *Warrior Bride* and was praised by authors and critics alike. Now, with *Virgin Bride*, she offers another electrifying tale of a woman who would give anything to avoid being sent to a convent—even her virtue.

❏ *56536-2 $5.50/6.99 in Canada*

Bestselling Women's Fiction

Sandra Brown

_____	28951-9 TEXAS! LUCKY	$5.99/6.99 in Canada
_____	28990-X TEXAS! CHASE	$5.99/6.99
_____	29500-4 TEXAS! SAGE	$5.99/6.99
_____	29085-1 22 INDIGO PLACE	$5.99/6.99
_____	29783-X A WHOLE NEW LIGHT	$5.99/6.99
_____	56045-X TEMPERATURES RISING	$5.99/6.99
_____	56274-6 FANTA C	$4.99/5.99
_____	56278-9 LONG TIME COMING	$4.99/5.99

Amanda Quick

_____	28354-5 SEDUCTION	$5.99/6.99
_____	28932-2 SCANDAL	$5.99/6.99
_____	28594-7 SURRENDER	$5.99/6.99
_____	29325-7 RENDEZVOUS	$5.99/6.99
_____	29316-8 RECKLESS	$5.99/6.99
_____	29316-8 RAVISHED	$4.99/5.99
_____	29317-6 DANGEROUS	$5.99/6.99
_____	56506-0 DECEPTION	$5.99/7.50

Nora Roberts

_____	29078-9 GENUINE LIES	$5.99/6.99
_____	28578-5 PUBLIC SECRETS	$5.99/6.99
_____	26461-3 HOT ICE	$5.99/6.99
_____	26574-1 SACRED SINS	$5.99/6.99
_____	27859-2 SWEET REVENGE	$5.99/6.99
_____	27283-7 BRAZEN VIRTUE	$5.99/6.99
_____	29597-7 CARNAL INNOCENCE	$5.50/6.50
_____	29490-3 DIVINE EVIL	$5.99/6.99

Iris Johansen

_____	29871-2 LAST BRIDGE HOME	$4.50/5.50
_____	29604-3 THE GOLDEN BARBARIAN	$4.99/5.99
_____	29244-7 REAP THE WIND	$4.99/5.99
_____	29032-0 STORM WINDS	$4.99/5.99
_____	28855-5 THE WIND DANCER	$4.95/5.95
_____	29968-9 THE TIGER PRINCE	$5.50/6.50
_____	29944-1 THE MAGNIFICENT ROGUE	$5.99/6.99
_____	29945-X BELOVED SCOUNDREL	$5.99/6.99

Ask for these titles at your bookstore or use this page to order.

Please send me the books I have checked above. I am enclosing $ _____ (add $2.50 to cover postage and handling). Send check or money order, no cash or C. O. D.'s please.

Mr./ Ms. _____

Address _____

City/ State/ Zip _____

Send order to: Bantam Books, Dept. FN 16, 2451 S. Wolf Road, Des Plaines, IL 60018

Please allow four to six weeks for delivery.

Prices and availability subject to change without notice.

FN 16 - 4/94